THE SADDLE CLUB

Horse Games

Bonnie Bryant

BANTAM BOOKS
TORONTO · NEW YORK · LONDON · SYDNEY · AUCKLAND

I would like to express special appreciation to Linda Kiss, who got me
started on this book, and to Pat Lebs, president of the American
Polocrosse Association, who helped me complete it. They each provided
me with information and enthusiasm.
Thank you both.

THE SADDLE CLUB: HORSE GAMES
A BANTAM BOOK 0 553 40436 9

First published in USA by Bantam Skylark Books
First publication in Great Britain

PRINTING HISTORY
Bantam edition published 1991

"The Saddle Club" is a trademark of Bonnie Bryant Hiller. The Saddle
Club design/logo, which consists of an inverted U-shaped design, a riding
crop, and a riding hat, is a trademark of Bantam Books.

With thanks to Suzanne's Riding School, Harrow Weald, for their help
in the preparation of the cover.

Bantam Books are published by Transworld Publishers Ltd.,
61-63 Uxbridge Road, Ealing, London W5 5SA, in Australia by
Transworld Publishers (Australia) Pty. Ltd., 15-23 Helles
Avenue, Moorebank, NSW 2170, and in New Zealand by Transworld
Publishers (N.Z.) Ltd., Cnr. Moselle and Waipareira Avenues,
Henderson, Auckland.

Made and printed in Great Britain by
The Guernsey Press Co. Ltd., Guernsey, Channel Islands.

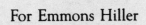

For Emmons Hiller

Phil Marston thinks he's such a hotshot rider! Like he invented the whole idea of riding!

Stevie Lake stormed along the roadside. Her dark blond hair bounced with each determined step. The Phil Marston in her thoughts was her boyfriend. Most of the time, they were very good friends. They felt the same way about a lot of things. The exception was deciding which one was the better horseback rider.

He even thinks he's better than I am. We'll show him!

The *we* in her thoughts included her two best friends, Carole Hanson and Lisa Atwood. Carole and Lisa rode horses at the same stable where Stevie was headed right now, Pine Hollow. The three of them loved horses and riding—and each other—so much that they called themselves The Saddle Club.

At that moment, Stevie was forgetting that they had invited Phil Marston to be in The Saddle Club. At that moment, Stevie was, in fact, forgetting everything about Phil Marston, except that he had just been telling her on the telephone about a new sport his Pony Club was playing. It was called polocrosse.

She'd been excited when he'd started to tell her about the sport.

"It's a combination of polo and lacrosse," he'd said. "You play with three horseback riders on a side in a big rectangular field with goalposts on either end."

"This sounds great," Stevie had said.

"It is," Phil had agreed. "Each player has a position, and the positions are numbered. The number 1 player is Attack, number 2 is the Center, and number 3 is Defense. Only Attack can score goals. I've been playing Attack. The teams we've played against so far really haven't been very good. I've scored a lot of goals."

Stevie could hear the unspoken challenge in Phil's description of the game. He wanted to play against a *good* team. Stevie thought that would be a fine idea. She wanted him to play against a good team, too, only she wanted to be on that good team and she wanted Phil's team to lose to it!

"He won't think he's such a hotshot for long!" she whispered under her breath as she entered the stable. She was so intent on her conversation with herself that she didn't notice Max Regnery, her riding instructor, directly in front of her. She walked right smack into him.

"Who won't what?" Max asked, grabbing her by the shoulders before they both fell down.

"Oh, sorry! I guess I—oh, wow! Max! Just the person I need to see. Can we talk?"

"Looks like this must be important," he said. "Sure, come on into my office."

CAROLE SNEEZED. ALMOST instantly, her father's hand came over and brushed her forehead. She knew he was sort of pretending that it was just a touch of affection, but she also knew he was really feeling for a fever. Reassured, he casually smoothed her shiny black hair and his hand returned to the steering wheel.

"I'm okay, Dad. I really am."

"That's the second time you've sneezed this morning," Colonel Hanson reminded her. He turned the car off the highway and onto the road that led to Pine Hollow Stables.

"There must be some dust in the car," she said. "I don't have a cold. I promise you."

"It's just that I care," he said.

"I know," Carole said. "But I'm okay, I really am. And even if something were wrong, the most healing thing in the world for me is horseback riding, and I'd only get sicker if I had to miss the Pony Club meeting today."

"So you are sick," he said instantly.

"No," Carole said, annoyed with herself for having invited further speculation. "I'm healthy as a horse."

Colonel Hanson glanced sideways at his daughter and smiled. He then turned his attention back to the road. Carole sighed with relief. Although she was convinced that he was just about the best father a girl could have, he did have his faults. He'd go through periods when he'd pay too much attention to her and worry too much about her. This was one of those periods.

In a way, Carole understood it. Her mother had died of cancer almost two years earlier and her father still worried that he should have known and should have done something earlier than he did. He turned his worry to Carole and expressed it with concern for her. Most of the time, Carole didn't mind, but when it threatened to interfere with her horseback riding, she minded a lot.

"HAVE YOU SEEN Stevie?" Lisa asked when Carole arrived at Pine Hollow. Lisa was in the middle of tacking up Pepper, the horse she usually rode.

"No, but her backpack is in her cubby in the locker area, so she must be here," Carole said.

"Max's office door is closed," Lisa said. "Do you think something's wrong?"

Carole scrunched her face in thought. Max was serious about riding and thought it was a great privilege. When his students didn't behave, or when their grades at school

4

slipped, Max would suspend their privileges. Stevie, whose idea of "fun" was not always within Max's definition of "behave," spent an awful lot of time in Max's office "explaining." She was good at explaining. At her young years, she'd already had a lifetime of experience explaining.

Carole shrugged. "I don't think he could have found out about the spilled soda in Veronica's cubby."

"Cross your fingers," Lisa said.

"I will, but it makes it hard to tack up a horse!" Carole joked.

"Horse Wise will come to attention in ten minutes!" the P.A. system warned.

Horse Wise was the name of their Pony Club, and ten minutes wasn't a lot of time to tack up a horse and get ready for the meeting.

Carole waved her hand, fingers still crossed, at Lisa, uttered a quick "See you!" and headed for the tack room. Lisa turned her attention to Pepper. She tugged his forelock out from under the crownpiece of his bridle and smoothed it for him.

When she was finished with that, she lifted Pepper's saddle onto his back and slid it into place. She checked to make sure the saddle pad was smooth.

"Hi, Lisa," Stevie greeted her, dashing past Pepper's stall, carrying Topside's tack.

"Hey, Stevie, what's up?" Lisa called after her.

"See you at Horse Wise!" was her only answer.

It was enough, though. As long as Stevie was going to be at the meeting, it meant either she'd never been in trouble, or she'd explained her way out of it. Lisa finished tacking up Pepper and hurried to the meeting.

All Horse Wise mounted meetings began with inspection. Stevie was a little worried about that. She'd been in such a hurry to tack up Topside she wasn't even positive she'd gotten his saddle on frontward. She glanced down. It was okay. Her bridle, however, wasn't. Topside used a full bridle with two reins and she'd gotten the leathers twisted. Today, of all days, she didn't want to delay the beginning of the real meeting. She leaned forward and untwined them as quickly as she could.

"Ready for inspection?" Max asked.

"I am now," she said, smiling.

Max smiled back weakly. "Proceed to the meeting," he said, approving her tack. She and Topside entered the outdoor ring.

A few minutes later, Max appeared with the final rider and the meeting began.

"Today," Max said, "we are going to learn a new game. It's called polocrosse."

Stevie almost cheered out loud. She wanted to tell everybody what had happened. It had been very eerie to appear in Max's office to talk about polocrosse only to find that he had already bought the equipment, marked off the field, and was planning to teach it to Horse Wise this very same day. It was just great. All they'd need to do was to have a few practice sessions and then they could compete with Phil's team—and beat them, of course! She'd show him a thing or two about scoring points. He'd see!

Carole had already heard about polocrosse, but she'd never played it or seen it being played. She watched with excitement as Max displayed the equipment: a rubber ball about the size of a softball, and a long-handled racquet with a shallow net used to scoop up, carry, and throw the ball.

"This is going to be great!" she whispered to Lisa, who was next to her in line at the meeting.

"Just three people play on each side at a time?" Lisa whispered back.

"Three's always been enough for us, hasn't it?" Carole asked.

Lisa smiled, remembering that three was, indeed, a very special number for The Saddle Club.

"Are you listening or talking?" Max asked, glaring at Carole and Lisa.

"Listening," they answered in a single voice. Then they turned their full attention to everything he was saying.

"This is what the field looks like," Max said, pointing to a chart that he had tacked to the fence of the ring. "All six players are allowed in the center area. Only Attack and Defense—from opposite teams, of course—are allowed in the goal-scoring areas. There's one at each end of the field, behind the penalty line. Attack must be in the goal-scoring area to score, and nobody can carry the ball over the penalty line. They have to throw it to another player on the other side of the line, or bounce it and pick it up themselves—like dribbling in basketball. Got it?"

"Can the Attack just carry the ball into the goal?" Lisa asked.

"Good question," Max said. "And the answer is no. The ball has to be thrown or bounced between the goalposts, and the Attack is not allowed closer to the goalposts than eleven yards. There's a large semicircle marked on the ground around the goal. So, now, you've got the general idea. Who wants to try it first?"

Every single hand went up.

Max regarded his riders studiously. His eyes darted around. Lisa could feel her excitement rising. She really wanted to play.

"Well, that's good news," Max said, "because we need twelve players. Six will be on each team, with three playing at a time. What we have here is twelve volunteers."

Within minutes, Max had six players on the field that adjoined the ring. Stevie, Lisa, and Carole were all on the same team, but they were going to play the second "chukka," as Max told them the six-minute periods were called.

"Go, Blue!" Stevie shouted encouragement to her teammates on the field.

"Max hasn't even tossed out the ball," Carole said. "Why are you yelling already?"

"Because we need to encourage our teammates to do the best they can," Stevie told her. "I was talking to Phil this morning and he told me about this game. The really funny thing is that at practically the same time I decided I had to learn it, Max had decided the same thing—"

"That *you* had to learn it?" Lisa teased.

"No—that all of us had to learn it, of course. Anyway, I can't let Phil go on thinking all his life that he's this super polocrosse player, you know?"

Carole and Lisa exchanged doubting looks. When Phil and Stevie had first met at riding camp, their friendship had almost been ruined by the competition between them.

"Are we looking at another bout of 'I can do anything better than he can'?" Lisa asked Carole.

"Sounds like it to me," Carole said. "Let's ask her."

Stevie glanced at both her friends. "Don't be silly," she said. "It's just that he was boasting and I hate it when he does that."

"I don't know," Carole said. "I'm not so sure you hate it when Phil says he's better at something than you are. What I think you hate is when you think he might be right."

The moment Carole said that, she was sorry. It wasn't that it wasn't true. It was just that she knew Stevie didn't want to hear it.

9

"Shows how much you know," Stevie said.

"Okay, second squads!" Max called out.

Stevie kicked Topside and pulled away from her friends.

"Saved by the instructor," Lisa said to Carole when Stevie was out of earshot.

"Maybe," Carole said, but it turned out that Lisa was right. Stevie's burst of temper at Carole disappeared almost as suddenly as it had arrived, for as soon as the three got onto the playing field, Stevie's attention was focused on mastering a new sport. She was too busy to be angry.

Max gave each of the girls a number. Stevie was 1, so her position was Attack. Lisa was 2—the Center. Carole was 3, Defense. He handed them each a racquet, lined them up next to the other team, and tossed out the ball.

"Got it!" Stevie yelled, but she didn't have it at all. The other team's Attack had it. Before Stevie could even get Topside turned around to try to get the ball from the Red Attack, he'd passed it to his Center. Lisa rode hard, trying to catch up with the Center, reaching for Red Center's stick, to hit it upward with her own. That was the way Max had told them they could get the ball from another player.

Lisa reached out and flailed at Red Center's stick with hers. She wasn't even close.

"Get it!" Stevie screamed.

"I can't!" Lisa screamed back.

"I can!" Stevie yelled with determination.

She then proceeded to dash after Red Center, waving her racquet as she approached.

The whistle blew.

"You can't threaten another rider with a racquet," Max scolded Stevie. "Remember, you can attack the ball, but not the ballcarrier."

Stevie nodded. Play resumed.

It seemed impossible to Lisa that the chukka was only six minutes long. How could it be that the players could make so many mistakes in six minutes? In that very short time, the ball was tossed out-of-bounds five times, and absolutely lost twice. On two occasions, five riders had chased one rider into the scoring area only to find that none of them had the ball, or even had any idea where it was!

The whistle blew.

"Whew!" Lisa said. The chukka had been fun, but it had been very hard. She was pretty sure her friends were feeling the same way she was, but she was wrong.

"Wasn't it wonderful?" Carole asked, clearly exhilarated.

"Boy, have you guys got a lot of work to do so we can beat Phil's Pony Club!" Stevie said.

Sometimes it amazed Lisa how three girls could be such good friends and so different all at once.

2

"I'LL JUST BE a minute, Dad," Carole said, hopping out of the car. She picked up Crystal's teddy bear and entered the children's hospital. Max had asked her to do this as a favor to him, but, really, it was something Carole was glad to do. A few weeks earlier, Carole had been running pony-cart rides for patients at the hospital during a festival sponsored by Stevie's school. She hadn't noticed when five-year-old Crystal left her bear under one of the seats. Max had come across it and asked Carole if she remembered to whom it belonged. There was no way Carole could forget the frightened little girl who clutched her teddy bear getting into the cart—or the excited and smiling child who got off the cart a few minutes later. Returning Crystal's teddy was more like a special honor than a favor.

Crystal was sleeping when Carole entered her hospital room. She looked so peaceful and contented that Carole couldn't bring herself to wake Crystal up. Instead, she put the teddy bear by the sleeping child's arms. Instinctively, Crystal hugged the stuffed animal and drew him to her chest. A smile crossed the child's face. Carole smiled, too, and tiptoed out of the room.

"Hi, there." A familiar voice greeted her as she approached the elevator. The words were warm, but the tone was oddly flat and ironic. "Have you come to spread more cheer?" Carole turned. It took her a second to recognize the girl who was talking to her. Then it came to her.

"Oh, hi," Carole said. "I remember you. Marie Dana, right?" Carole was trying to sound casual, but the fact was, she couldn't forget the girl. When she'd seen her at the festival, Marie had been confined to a gurney—a stretcher on wheels. She'd had to lie absolutely flat on her back because of a broken pelvis. She'd been grumpy and almost rude at the festival. Now, she was up and walking, with the help of some crutches. Carole hoped that was improving her mood, too. "Looks like you're getting better, huh?"

"I guess that's what it *looks* like," Marie said. From the way she said it, Carole knew that although her physical state was clearly better, emotionally she had not improved.

That was what Carole remembered the most about

her. Marie had resisted all attempts to help her. It was almost as if she were determined to be unhappy.

"Are you still in the hospital now?" Carole asked.

"No. I'm just here for physical therapy. It's something they make me do four times a week to keep my mind on how much it hurts to walk."

Carole laughed. Marie smiled weakly in spite of herself.

"Are you still running pony-cart rides?" Marie asked.

"No, that was just for the day," Carole said. "But I am riding a lot. In fact, I just came from there."

"I know," Marie said. She pointed to Carole.

Carole looked down and then blushed. No wonder Marie could tell she'd been riding. She was still wearing breeches and high boots. Her riding gloves poked out of her pocket. The only thing that was missing was her hard hat.

"It's sort of a giveaway, isn't it?" she said.

"Yeah," said Marie.

There was a *bing* then, and the elevator arrived. Carole stepped on first and held the door while Marie walked on slowly, using crutches.

There were a lot of other people on the elevator. Carole didn't feel like talking as they rode down, stopping at almost every floor. She stood quietly, but her eyes watched Marie's back and her mind raced. There was a very special quality about Marie. Carole didn't know what it was, but she instinctively recognized that they had things in common and that Marie wanted to talk to her. Marie's sharp tongue and grumpiness couldn't hide the fact that she needed a friend. Carole wondered if she could be the friend and, if she could, what good it would do Marie.

The elevator drew to a stop at the ground floor. Marie stepped off slowly. Carole followed her.

"Is somebody meeting you?" Carole asked. "I mean, my dad is waiting for me outside. We could give you a lift."

"No thanks. I just finished up my therapy a little early today, so my mother isn't here yet. That's funny, too, because since the accident, she's barely wanted to let me out of her sight."

"Is she afraid it will happen again?" Carole asked. She was trying to make a little joke out of it. After all, she knew what it was like to have a parent who sometimes cared too much.

"No, I don't think so," Marie said. "It's more like she's afraid she'll lose me, too. See, my father was killed in the same accident that put me in the hospital."

That was it, then. That was what Carole had intuitively sensed that was their common bond. They had each had a parent die, Carole's mother from cancer, Marie's father in an accident. Carole wanted to say something, but an odd thing happened. She and Marie had the most important thing in the world in common and she didn't know what to say. She didn't know how to tell her that she really did know how much it hurt. Sharing her own sadness didn't seem like the right thing to do just then.

"I'm sorry," was all Carole said. "Really."

"Thanks," Marie said. Then she winced and Carole got the feeling her legs were hurting her.

"Want to sit down a minute?" Carole asked.

Marie nodded. Carole led her to a bench in the lobby of the hospital and sat down next to her. It was an awkward moment. There was a lot Carole wanted to say and even more she wanted to ask, but she had the feeling that Marie didn't want to talk about what she had just told Carole. Carole switched the subject to the one she always felt the most comfortable with.

"Have you ever done any horseback riding?"

Marie laughed. "That's funny," she said.

Carole didn't think it was funny at all. She certainly hadn't meant to be funny. "How's that?" she asked.

"Well, you're the second person to ask me that in just a few minutes. The therapist upstairs wanted to know, too."

"And what's the answer?" Carole asked expectantly.

"I guess it's yes. I used to ride before the accident. Not much, just a little," she said.

"Did you like it?" Carole asked, though even as she asked it, she thought it was a strange question. She, herself, could not imagine not liking horseback riding.

"Sure," Marie said. "You like it a lot, don't you?"

"Yes," Carole said. She was inspired by the question. "It's about the most important thing in the world to me. I love horseback riding. I love horses. I even have my own horse. My dad gave him to me for Christmas. His name is Starlight. He's a bay and he's got this beautiful star right on his face. He's pretty young and I've been working on finishing his training. I think he's going to be wonderful. Someday, I hope I'll be able to ride him in shows. I know he'll win—though I don't know about me, of course. Anyway, he's terrific. You should meet him sometime. Would you like to?"

"What do you like better? Riding or talking about it?" Marie asked.

Carole smiled. "I know. My friends tell me that when I get started talking about horses and riding, there's no stopping me. I'm sorry. I didn't mean to be boring. It's just that I think riding is wonderful. Everything about horses is wonderful. I mean, I even like it when I have to groom Starlight or take care of him in any way. I suppose that sounds weird, but, when you think about it, having a horse is a lot of responsibility as well as fun and the responsibility sort of makes the fun all the more—" She stopped abruptly. "Am I doing it again?"

"Yes," Marie said, now almost laughing. It wasn't a mean laugh, though. It was more like a friendly laugh.

"I think I'm incorrigible," Carole said. "But I don't mind. I like myself that way."

"It's okay," Marie said. "I don't mind, either."

Just then a woman waved to Marie. The girl waved back. "My mother," she said, though it wasn't necessary. Marie looked just like her. Mrs. Dana was tall and slender. Her dark eyes were wide-set and bright. When she smiled the greeting to her daughter, Carole realized how pretty Marie would be if she ever smiled as broadly as her mother did.

"Done already? Did it go okay? What did the therapist say?" Mrs. Dana shot questions at her daughter faster than Marie could have answered them if she'd wanted to.

"Everything's fine, Mom," Marie said. "Let's go." Then, with some effort, the girl stood up using her crutches to help and followed her mother through the hospital lobby and out the doorway.

Carole waved and called good-bye to the Danas. Marie acknowledged it with a nod.

"See you," Carole called.

Marie nodded again, this time more faintly.

Carole went out to her father's car, opened the door, and got in. She expected him to be annoyed at how long it had taken her to return Crystal's teddy bear, but found instead that he was curious about who she'd been with.

"Oh, that's a girl I met at the festival thing. She's not staying in the hospital anymore. She was just there for some therapy."

"And what about the woman with her?" her father persisted.

"That's Marie's mother, Dad," Carole said.

"Oh," he said, a little disappointed.

It took Carole a few seconds to figure out why her father sighed after he said "Oh." Then it struck her.

"She's a widow, Dad," Carole explained.

"Oh," he said more brightly.

"Her husband was killed in an automobile accident at the same time Marie got hurt."

"Hmmmmm," he said.

"Were you annoyed that I took so long?" she asked.

"No," he said. "I was just concerned that you might have gotten sick and decided to stay there. And, by the way, how are you feeling? Any more sign of that fever you had earlier today?"

"I never did have a fever, Dad," Carole said.

"But you were sick this morning," he reminded her.

"No. You just *thought* I was sick. I'm in fine shape—healthy as a—"

"I remember," he said. "You're healthy as a horse. Just see to it you stay that way, okay?"

"Deal," she said. She took his hand, which was resting on the seat of the car, and squeezed it. Sometimes it was a nuisance having a father who could start worrying about you at any moment. Most of the time it wasn't a nuisance at all.

"HELLO?" STEVIE'S VOICE sounded sweet and cheery. It wasn't exactly the way she felt, but it was the way she wanted a certain telephone caller to *think* she felt.

"Hi, it's me," Phil Marston said.

"Oh, wow, hi," Stevie said. No matter what she was scheming, the sound of Phil's voice was always welcome and she couldn't help her enthusiasm. "I was hoping you'd call. Wait until I tell you what we did today in Pony Club."

Phil waited. Stevie went on. "We actually learned how to play polocrosse. Can you believe it? I mean, after all, we were just talking about that earlier and *boom* that's the very next activity Max had for us. It was a blast—just like you said it would be."

"What position were you playing?"

"Attack," Stevie said, trying to sound casual.

"Score many goals?" he asked.

"We only played one chukka," she told him.

"Score any goals?" he asked.

"Just four—or was it five?" Stevie knew perfectly well that the answer was four, not five. And she also knew that that was the total number scored by both teams the entire day. Of those, two were disqualified because Attack was too close to the goal, another was disqualified because the ball had been carried over the penalty line, and the fourth wasn't anything to boast about because it had been made in the team's home goal. Stevie had not been personally responsible for any of those disasters. Her own goal attempt had missed completely. The ball had flown out of her racquet, off the playing field, and into the stable, startling three horses and a stablehand. Stevie didn't think she needed to mention that.

"Hey, that's pretty good for your first time at polocrosse," Phil said.

"Oh, I don't know. I think we're going to get a lot better." She certainly hoped so, anyway!

"Probably," he said. "Practice makes a lot of difference in a game like polocrosse."

"Well, maybe," Stevie said. She didn't actually doubt that he was right and she knew that her team would have to do a lot of practicing very soon, but she needed to take another angle right then. "Sometimes, though, I think if you simply practice with other people who are new at something, you just study mistakes. The best thing would be to actually play against somebody really good. Do you know anybody really good that we could learn from?"

"I'm not sure I've ever heard of any other team's Attack that scored four or five goals in one chukka the first time it practiced," Phil said. "I mean, what's the point of trying to learn from somebody else when you're already that good?"

Of all the nerve. He was as good as calling her a liar.

"You don't believe me?" Stevie said.

"I didn't say that," he protested, but she knew he didn't believe her and it annoyed her. It didn't occur to her right then that he had a very good reason for not believing her and that was because what she'd said simply wasn't true.

"Well, if you don't think we're very good, why don't you just give us a chance to show you? I mean, all you have to do is bring a team over to Pine Hollow and you can see for yourself!"

"I might just do that," Phil said. "As a matter of fact, there's going to be a Pony Club rally in two weeks. Why don't you ask Max if he thinks Horse Wise can compete against my club? I'll talk to my team and see if they are interested in showing you guys a thing or two. . . ."

That was just what Stevie had been hoping for. She knew that if she boasted about how good they were, Phil would have to rise to the challenge and agree to a match.

"Done," she said. "I'll talk to Max on Tuesday."

"I'll call my instructor right now," Phil said. "I'll talk to you again next week—unless you're too busy practicing to come to the phone!"

That's just like Phil, Stevie thought. He was *so* competitive!

CAROLE PUT DOWN her book to answer the phone. She didn't have much idea of what she'd been reading anyway. Her mind had been on Marie Dana, not her book report.

"Hi, Carole, I'm glad you're there. Have I got something to tell you."

It was Stevie, of course. Nobody else jumped into a phone conversation the way she did.

"Hi, what's up?" It was impossible not to be drawn in by Stevie's enthusiasm, no matter what it was about.

"Well, I just talked to Phil, and—guess what?"

"He's taking you to opening night at the opera on Thursday?" Carole teased.

"Huh? Oh, no. It's much better than that. He's going to talk to his Pony Club instructor and see if they can play us in a polocrosse match at the next rally."

"This is exciting?" Carole asked. "You thought his ego needed some sort of gigantic boost?"

"What do you mean?" Stevie sounded indignant.

"We're going to lose badly. We don't know what we're doing out there," Carole said.

"But that was just today. Wait until we've had a couple of practices. I mean, we are better riders. We know that."

"You don't mean 'we,' you mean you. Personally, I don't care if I'm a better rider than Phil Marston. He's a good rider and he takes care of his horse. That's all that matters, isn't it?"

"But he thinks he's this *great* rider and he was so impressed with himself, telling me about all the goals he scored when he was Attack and all the ones he prevented when he was Defense. I just thought we ought to take him down a peg or two."

Stevie wasn't making an awful lot of sense. Sometimes she was like that, Carole knew. Although most of the time Stevie was quite sane, the fact was that she was very competitive—even when there wasn't anything to be competitive about (like her own polocrosse "skills"). It was a lesson Stevie had learned before, though it didn't seem to have stayed with her.

"Don't you think so?" Stevie persisted.

Carole thought about it for a few seconds. "Well, I know it would be fun to play against Phil's team. They may not be wonderful, but they do have some experience, so it would be good for us—"

"I knew you'd agree," Stevie said. "I'll ask Max about it on Tuesday after class. I know he'll say yes, too. Right now, though, I'm going to call Lisa and tell her what we're planning. She won't believe it, either. Isn't it wonderful?"

Before Carole had a chance to answer, Stevie had hung up. Carole regarded her phone quizzically and laughed. Stevie was like that—especially when she got a

24

bee in her bonnet, and polocrosse had definitely put one there! There was no way to talk sense to Stevie when she was in one of those moods. Besides, experience had shown Carole and Lisa that more often than not, things actually ended up working out the way Stevie wanted them to, though often not quite as she had planned.

Carole had the feeling that they would be learning an awful lot about polocrosse in the next few weeks. She didn't mind. Although they'd been dreadful in their practice this afternoon, polocrosse was played on horseback, and anything on horseback had a terrific advantage over anything not on horseback.

Riding had always been a wonderful, fun, exciting, and comforting activity for Carole. In fact, she sometimes wondered how she would have made it through the pain and sadness of her mother's illness and death without the constant comfort of riding. Even when things were very tough, she always felt better on horseback. The recollection of her own difficult experiences made her think of Marie. Carole really did know how Marie was feeling. She just wished Marie could get the same help from horseback riding that she'd gotten. And then she wondered, *Why not?*

Carole's mind began churning. Wouldn't it be wonderful, she thought, to be able to share horseback riding with somebody else who needed it as much as she had once. What better thing could one friend do for another? But how could she do it?

Carole wasn't a schemer. She wasn't one to come up with clever plans to talk people into doing things they didn't know they wanted to do. On the other hand, Carole knew somebody who was a master at doing that. She paused for a moment and asked herself the obvious question: "What would Stevie do?"

Stevie would get on the phone. First she'd call Miss Bellanger, the head administrator at the hospital, to get Marie's address and to ask if horseback riding would be okay for her. Then, she'd figure out a way to entice Marie to try riding at Pine Hollow. That's how Stevie would do it and that, Carole decided, was how she would do it, too.

ONE OF THE best things about owning a horse was that it needed to be exercised almost every day. Carole had her riding lessons on Tuesdays and Horse Wise Pony Club on Saturdays. On the other days, whenever she could, she'd go straight to Pine Hollow after school and take Starlight out. It also gave her a chance to groom him and feed him. Time spent with Starlight was wonderful no matter what she was doing.

She tightened the buckle of his girth one more notch and led him to the door of the stable that led out onto the paths through the fields. She mounted up, touched the good-luck horseshoe, and was off. Today was special. She wasn't just going to go for a ride; she had a mission.

Carole could still recall Miss Bellanger's excitement

over the phone. The hospital had been trying to get Marie to take up horseback riding because it would be good for her legs. Marie, however, had been resisting suggestions for anything that would be good for her. Carole wasn't surprised. She just hoped she could help. "Good luck!" Miss Bellanger had said.

The other good news was that Marie lived right near Pine Hollow. Her family's house was just across the field behind the stable. Carole and her friends had ridden near there many times. Carole even knew which house it was. It seemed odd to her that somebody could live so close to Pine Hollow and not ride, but then, not everybody was born loving horses the way Carole had been.

"Come on, boy!" she said to Starlight once they were through the first gate. He nodded his head eagerly, flicked his ears to be alert to anything going on around him, and then began trotting.

Carole loved trotting. It was a pace a horse could keep up for a long time, but it was fast enough that it wasn't boring. She would have loved to just trot straight across the field to Marie's house, but she had some work to do first. Starlight was a young horse and he hadn't really finished his training. Carole knew it was important to work with him and teach him something every single time they rode, no matter how much they each would have preferred to do something else.

The problem right then was that Carole hadn't told Starlight to trot. She'd told him to walk. She'd given him the signal with her legs, her seat, and her reins. Instead, he'd decided he wanted to trot. She couldn't let him get away with that.

"Whoa!" she said, reining him in. He halted. That was a good sign. She made him stand still for a few seconds before she tried again. Then she nudged him with her legs, shifted her weight in the saddle and relaxed her hold on the reins. He began walking. "Good boy," she told him. Then she told him the same thing with her hands by relaxing the reins a little bit more. He continued walking. After a few more steps, she signaled him to trot. He trotted immediately. That was good, and she once again told him with her voice and her hands. Then she told him to slow to a walk. He stopped.

It took Carole a while, but with a few more reminders to Starlight about which signal meant which gait, he seemed back in the groove. Once again, she took him through his paces: walk, trot, canter, trot, canter, walk, trot, stop.

"Good boy," she said, and then leaned forward to pat him on his neck. Once again, he nodded his head. She was sure he knew how pleased she was with him, just as she'd been sure he'd known that he was just being naughty before.

"Okay, that's enough schooling for you for today," she told him. "Now we've got somebody else who has a few things to learn. Ready?"

His ears flicked around again, alert to the change of tone in her voice, ready for another signal.

She began at a walk and then reached behind the girth with her left foot, touching his belly gently. He knew that signal; it was one of his favorites. He began cantering across the field.

Starlight had the most wonderful rocking canter Carole had ever known in a horse. It was fast and it was smooth. She felt the wind brush her hair and watched the countryside as she passed by. She kept a fairly tight rein on Starlight and directed him carefully, never letting him forget who was actually in charge.

As they neared the far side of the field, Carole drew her horse to a walk. He needed to cool down a bit and it wasn't a good idea to have a horse cantering on somebody's lawn. Soon the two of them left the field and approached Marie's house.

Carole and Starlight circled the house. The name Dana on the mailbox confirmed that it was the right house. There was no car in the driveway, but it wasn't the right time of day for Marie's therapy. Carole felt sure she must be home.

Carole looked at the house carefully. It was a nice, well-kept home. There was a picture window looking out from what she assumed was the living room. Then, in the room next to that, she could see a chandelier hanging from the ceiling. It looked like the dining room.

Beyond that was the kitchen. That was the whole down-stairs and Carole didn't see any signs of life on the ground floor. Her eyes moved to the upper floor. There were sev-eral windows with sheer white curtains. They had to be bedrooms. Was Marie somewhere inside? Was she look-ing out? Did she see Carole? How could she *miss* Carole? There was no movement.

Carole and Starlight continued around the house. Just as they reached the corner, Carole thought she noticed a slight movement in one of the curtains. Marie? Maybe, she told herself. Maybe it was a little bit of breeze, too.

Then, just around the corner, another curtain moved aside, ever so slightly. Carole was certain now it was Marie. She was just as certain the girl wasn't going to say anything to Carole. It didn't matter. Carole had accom-plished what she'd wanted. She had made Marie curious enough to look—twice.

Carole believed firmly that horseback riding was an activity that had its own rewards and it should never be done to show off. She broke her own rule then.

Suddenly, she swung Starlight around, startled him with a kick, yelled "Yahoooooo!" like a cowboy, got her horse to gallop, and then jumped him over the low wooden fence at the back of the Dana's yard instead of going through the gate as they had done when they ar-rived. She didn't even let him slow down until she was sure they were out of sight of Marie's house.

"Sorry, boy," she said when Starlight was walking

slowly. "I know you like more warning than that, but I had my reasons. I promise you I did. And just because you were such a good boy and did exactly what I wanted you to do, I'm going to let you pick the next gait. It's your turn."

She loosened up on the reins. Starlight began trotting.

JUST ABOUT FIVE minutes before the start of the next
practice, Lisa had changed her mind about what fun it
was going to be to learn polocrosse. The problem could
be summed up in one word: Stevie.

After class on Tuesday, Max had lined up the riders
who stayed for practice, and had them all take turns picking up the ball, first on the right, then on the left. That
was fine. It was something they needed to practice. Most
of them weren't very good at it at first. Stevie, the first
person in the line, got to try it first. She wasn't very good
at it either. That didn't stop her from giving hints and
suggestions to the other riders as their turns came
around.

"No, no!" she yelled at Lisa. "You have to lean forward
as well as sideways to reach the ball!"

Lisa didn't thank her for the advice.

When they were trying to pick up the ball on the left-hand side of the horse, it was Carole's turn to get some advice.

"You can't change hands!" Stevie yelled. "That's not allowed. If you do that in a tournament, you'll get us a foul!"

It didn't make any difference that Stevie happened to be right. The way she delivered the message was so unpleasant that nobody wanted to listen to what she said.

Carole just slipped the racquet back into her right hand, reached over across Starlight's neck, stretched, and picked up the ball. She tossed it easily to Max, who caught it with his racquet and smiled. "Nice move," he said.

Lisa didn't know how Carole managed to refrain from glaring at Stevie.

"Next, we're going to try passing back and forth to one another."

He had the riders split into two groups and line their horses up facing each other, ten feet apart. They counted off. Evens on one side, odds on the other. He announced he would toss the ball to the closest rider, number 1, and explained that he wanted the riders to "lace" it—toss it numerically, 1 to 2 to 3, back and forth across the space, and then back down again to him. Eventually, he said, this would be a timed exercise.

That would have been fine except the number 1 rider,

Adam Levine, didn't catch the ball. He merely swiped up into the air with his racquet as the ball whizzed by and bounced down to the end of the field. Adam chased after the thing and tried four or five times to pick it up before he finally got it into his racquet. Then he threw it back, getting it only half the distance it needed to go. He had to pick it up again.

By that time, Stevie was beside herself. A number of the players were yelling encouragement, but Stevie was just plain yelling.

"Hurry up! We haven't got all day! The rest of us want a chance to practice, too!"

Finally, Adam picked up the ball and rode slowly back to his place in line. Some of the riders may have thought he was doing that to be careful so he wouldn't drop the ball again. Lisa was convinced he was doing it to irritate Stevie.

Then Adam tossed the ball to the number 2 rider, who also missed it. Most of the riders—including Stevie—missed it and had to chase it down. When they'd finished lacing the ball—all over the field—Max called them to attention.

"Right now, this exercise seems more like a chasing-down-and-picking-up exercise than a throwing-and-catching one. Don't worry. We all need practice with chasing down and picking up, too. The time has not gone to waste."

He said the last few words slowly, glaring directly at

Stevie. Lisa thought he was being a little bit too subtle for Stevie in her present mood, but there wasn't much even Max could do about it. The fact was, she told herself, hitting Stevie in the side of the head with a two-by-four might have been too subtle right then.

"Now, I want to try something else," Max said. "I want to try a practice chukka. We have accepted a challenge from Cross County Pony Club, and because of unforeseen scheduling problems, the match is going to take place on Saturday."

"This *weekend?*" Stevie screeched. "But we won't be ready. We'll never win!"

"No, I'm sure we won't," Max said quite calmly. "I wouldn't expect us to win our first match in any event. So, think of it as an intense practice rather than a real match."

Lisa suspected that that was more than Stevie could handle. It was clear, within a few seconds, that she was right. As soon as the practice chukka started, Stevie started too—on the players.

Lisa and Carole waited on the sidelines to be called in to play. Stevie was playing number 2, Center, for her team.

"It was bad enough when she thought the match against Phil's club was going to be in two weeks. Now that it's this week, there's no stopping her," Lisa complained.

"When Stevie gets an idea in her head—"

"I know, I know. Even an atom bomb can't blast it out. But if she doesn't stop being so awful to everybody, somebody's going to go to a lot of trouble to find an atom bomb somewhere . . ."

"If we don't just strangle her with our bare hands first." Carole finished the sentence for Lisa.

"Now there's an idea," Lisa said.

Although she was interested in learning polocrosse, and even interested in at least putting on a good show for Phil's team on Saturday, Carole just couldn't get herself to care as much as Stevie. Right then, something, or rather somebody, else seemed more important, and her name was Marie Dana. Under the circumstances, polocrosse just didn't seem very urgent.

"You seem to be involved with something," Lisa said, interrupting her thoughts. "It's as if you've already left practice."

Carole smiled. Lisa had a way, sometimes, of knowing what people were thinking, even before they did.

"I think you're right," she agreed. "I have, at least in my mind. Now I think I'm going to do it for real. Tell Stevie I'm sorry, will you?"

Before Lisa could protest, Carole had Starlight trotting across the field—toward Marie's.

"Carole?" Max said as she passed him. "Where are you going?"

"I've got to see somebody, Max. Right now."

"Okay," he said. Max wasn't the kind of person to pry.

36

Carole was glad of it. Right then, she wished she could have said the same for her friend Stevie.

"Where are you going?" Stevie demanded. "Practice isn't over, you know. There are five more minutes left and you can learn a lot from watching as well as doing. You can't just . . ."

But she did.

THE QUIET OF the fields between Pine Hollow and Marie's house was very welcome. Carole liked riding in any form, but being yelled at wasn't high on her hit parade. As soon as she was out of range of Stevie's voice, she wondered why she hadn't left earlier.

Things were still quiet at Marie's house. Again, there was no car in the driveway and the house was closed up. Carole and Starlight circled the house. Carole paused at the rear, where she'd seen Marie at the window the day before. She allowed Starlight to nibble on the green lawn while she examined the house. The movement of a curtain again caught Carole's eye. She squinted to focus with the afternoon sun blurring her vision. It took a second, but she saw Marie. The girl stood by the window and looked back at her. Carole waved. Marie just continued looking. Finally, she waved in return. Carole even thought she saw Marie smile.

It was so little, but it was so much. Carole was tempted to dismount and ring Marie's doorbell, but if she did that and Marie didn't answer, what would that mean? That she didn't want to open the door? That she couldn't? Carole decided not to raise the question.

She gave a final wave and, once again, she turned Starlight dramatically and galloped out of the Danas' yard and over the fence. This time, Starlight elected to walk back to Pine Hollow.

Carole was glad for that. She hoped that the polocrosse practice would be done, the horses groomed, and the riders departed by the time she got back. She was in luck. The place was almost deserted. She untacked Starlight, cleaned out his stall, and groomed him carefully. She also gave him his afternoon ration of grain and some fresh hay and water. He nodded his appreciation and nuzzled her neck when she gave him a carrot for a treat.

When she was sure he was all taken care of, she hefted his saddle and bridle and took them back to the tack room.

"That you, Carole?" Mrs. Reg asked from her office next door. Mrs. Reg was Max's mother and the business manager of the stable. She was also a sort of unofficial mother to anyone she thought might need mothering from time to time.

"Yes, it's me," Carole said.

"Max said you'd disappeared from the practice. Everything okay?"

"Yes ma'am," Carole told her. "I just had to go visit a friend. She's sick. And she lives in one of the houses on the other side of the fields."

"Hmmm," Mrs. Reg responded.

Carole lifted the saddle and put it on its rack. She straightened out the pad and made sure that the leathers were hanging straight. Then she untangled the bridle and hung it from its hook. As she was doing that, she saw that there was some mud on the bridle. It must have happened in polocrosse practice. She took it back down. It would only take her a second to clean it. She grabbed the saddle soap and a sponge and sat down to do the quick job.

Mrs. Reg came in and sat down beside her. "It's a good thing you're cleaning that now," she said. "If you wait until the next time you ride—"

"I know, I know," Carole said with a good-natured laugh. "If you clean your tack every day you'll never have a problem." She repeated what she had been told hundreds of times by Max and Mrs. Reg. She knew it was a good lesson.

"Well, some things have to be taken care of right away. Some things just take time, you know." Mrs. Reg picked up a sponge and began cleaning the other end of the bridle for Carole. She talked as she cleaned.

"Reminds me of a horse we had here once," Mrs. Reg began. She was famous for her stories. They always had to do with horses and riders from long ago, but they usually also had to do with a problem or a situation that was happening right then.

"This horse belonged to the stable," Mrs. Reg con-

tinued. "Max, my husband, just loved that guy. I sometimes thought it was because they were both stubborn.
He was an Appaloosa, bred for the rigors of the plains.
Anyway, he was one of the best trail horses we ever had.
He'd take riders out for hours at a time and never get
fussy or anything. At the end of a long trail ride, when
all the other horses would start hurrying to get back to
the barn, this old fellow would just walk at his own leisurely pace. Max sometimes even hurried him up, just to
see if he would act like the other horses, but it never
worked. Then Max would put him in his stall, groom
him and everything, and put a bucket of water in there
for him. All the other horses would guzzle their water.
Not this fellow."

Mrs. Reg finished the strap she was working on. She
put down her sponge and leaned forward, elbows on her
knees.

"Max got worried about how he wouldn't drink after a
long ride. Then one day, he asked the vet about it. The
vet said, 'When you get there in the morning, is the
water gone?' Max told him it was. 'Then what are you
worried about?'"

Mrs. Reg put her hands on her knees then and stood
up. The story was over—at least as much of it as Mrs.
Reg was going to tell. One of the most challenging things
about listening to Mrs. Reg's stories was figuring out what
they were really about. As Mrs. Reg returned to her of-

fice, Carole thought about the Appaloosa who wouldn't drink when his bucket was filled.

"Oh!" Carole said, suddenly getting it. *You can lead a horse to water, but you can't make him drink, and as long as he isn't getting dehydrated, leave him alone.* That had been easy. Next, she wanted to know how Mrs. Reg had known to give her that message right then.

STEVIE BOUNDED OUT of bed on Saturday morning. This was The Day! It was the day her Pony Club's polocrosse team would have a chance to show Phil Marston's team a thing or two—or meet total humiliation and defeat.

She went to the other window of her room. It was a bright and sunny spring day. There wasn't a cloud in the sky. Stevie's heart sank. She'd been dreaming all night that it would be pouring rain. Deep down, she had the worst feeling that the only way to avoid total humiliation would be for the match to be rained out.

Quickly, she swept the thought from her mind. That was a loser's way of thinking and would do her no good at all.

She washed and dressed and then went to the phone. One of the things she had to be sure of was that her best friends—and the Pony Club's best riders—would be there.

Unfortunately, she found that she woke up both Lisa and Carole, to say nothing of their parents. More than a little annoyed, they assured Stevie they did plan to be there and they would be on time. Stevie looked at her clock. It was seven-fifteen. She admitted to herself that maybe that was just a little bit early for a phone call on Saturday morning.

She took her polocrosse rule book, went down to the kitchen, and poured herself a bowl of cereal. She combed through the booklet to be sure she understood everything. The last thing she and her team needed was to commit fouls just because they didn't read this.

"SHE CALLED ME at seven-fifteen. What time did she call you?" Lisa asked Carole.

"Seven-ten. It's a good thing my father really likes her, too, because otherwise he would have hung up on her."

"And then she called again at eight-twenty to tell me that the only way you can try to get a ball out of an opponent's racquet is to hit the stick with an upward stroke," Lisa said.

"Did she tell you about left-handed players? That the team captain has to notify the opposing captain and the umpires in the event any of the players will be playing left-handed? I got that call at eight-thirty."

"But we don't have any left-handed players, do we?"

"Not anymore," Carole said. "Lorraine Olsen is left-handed, but she couldn't take Stevie's bullying and dropped out."

"I can't say that I blame her," Lisa said.

"It's tempting, isn't it?" Carole asked.

"I just keep reminding myself that Stevie's got this bright idea and it has to do with Phil and we should try to be understanding. After all, she is our best friend. And once the game is over, everything will change back. Won't it?"

"I hope so," Carole said. "I certainly hope so. And so does my dad."

"Horse Wise will now come to order in Max's office!" the P.A. barked, ending their conversation. They joined their teammates and the rest of the club in Max's office.

"You all know we're going to have a match today," Max began. "I want to tell you it's not a particularly important match. We're new at polocrosse and so is Cross County. Winning is nice, but playing our best is more important. We have all been working hard this week, and I know that we will do well, which doesn't always mean succeeding on the scoreboard. I want to wish all of the players good luck and to assure you that the rest of us will be on the sidelines cheering like crazy."

Carole thought Max's talk was just right. After all, they were there to have fun as much as to do well. She hoped that his words would have an effect on Stevie and help her to put the day into perspective.

"Can I say something, Max?" Stevie asked.

A look of doubt crossed Max's face, but he nodded his assent. Stevie stood up.

"I know I've been mean and awful this week." She paused because everybody was laughing. She probably didn't realize how true her words were. "I guess I've yelled at a few of you here."

Everybody's hand went up. Stevie seemed genuinely surprised, but had the grace to laugh. Carole thought the direction Stevie was taking was positively refreshing. It was hard to believe it was the same girl who'd called her twice before breakfast with "tips" for success.

"Well, it's true," she confessed. "Anyway, what happened, between the couple of practices we had, is that we got better. So, although it wasn't much fun, it worked and I'm beginning to get the feeling that we can really show those kids from Cross County who can play polocrosse and who can't. Let's go for it!"

A few of the Pony Clubbers started clapping. Stevie had turned the meeting into a pep rally and, Carole thought, maybe that wasn't a bad idea. After all, unpleasant as Stevie had been, they had learned some things. Maybe they did have a chance. Maybe.

The Cross County Pony Club was arriving at Pine Hollow with all its members and their horse vans by the time the Horse Wise members filed out of Max's office. Max greeted Mr. Baker, their instructor, and all the parent volunteers shook hands with one another and introduced themselves.

The Pony Clubbers stood apart and regarded one another warily. Stevie stood at the front of the pack of Horse Wise, Phil at the front of Cross County.

"Hi, Stevie," Phil said.

"Hello," Stevie returned.

Carole noticed that it was almost as if the two of them had never met before. The awkward moment passed quickly, though, because it was time for the teams to tack up and saddle up.

There were six players from Horse Wise. The agreement was that, just before the game began, they would draw numbers to determine squads and positions. Max showed them the cards. They read 1A, 2A, and 3A and 1B, 2B, and 3B. That would determine the A squad and the B squad and which position, Attack, Center, or Defense, would be played.

Max held out the hat with the cards for Horse Wise. Mr. Baker did the same for Cross County's team of six.

Carole unfolded her slip of paper. It read 3A. She showed it to her friends as they opened theirs. Somehow, it worked. The Saddle Club was on the same squad. Stevie was the Attack, Lisa the Center, and Carole the Defense. They would be playing at the same time. According to what Max said, the A squads would play the first and third chukkas, the B squads would play second and fourth.

"We'll have a chance to draw first blood!"

So much for Stevie's change of heart.

Stevie, Lisa, and Carole lined up across from Phil and two of his teammates, waiting for the umpire, Max, to toss in the ball, beginning the first six-minute chukka.

"Begin play!" Max announced. He threw the ball right between the rows of riders.

Phil picked it up first. He was the Attack for his team. He tossed it to his Center. Stevie was closest to the Center. She rode after him, reaching across the Center's horse to try to hit the Center's stick from below.

"Foul!"

Play stopped.

"Stevie, you can't reach across another rider's horse to try to get the ball out of an opponent's racquet," Max said.

"Oh, yeah," Stevie said, recalling the rule she'd read that very morning.

"Penalty free throw!" he announced.

The Cross County Center took the ball, tossed it to Phil across the penalty line, and he neatly tossed it right through the goalposts.

"Score!" Max called out.

"Huh?" Stevie said. It had happened so fast. First she'd made a mistake, then Phil's team had scored. Her own team hadn't even tried to defend against the goal attempt.

"Carole!" Stevie shrieked in anger. "What were you doing? You should have been there, and stopped it!"

"One nothing. Let's begin play!"

This time, Lisa managed to swat her racquet at the ball as it whizzed toward her. She did succeed in getting it down onto the ground, just in time for Cross County's Defense player to pick it up and pass it to their Center.

Carole saw trouble coming and headed for the goal area as fast as possible. Since Attack probably wasn't going to be a very important part of this game for her team, she suspected most of the work would be done by her as Defense—and not necessarily well.

She galloped Starlight down to the goal she was to defend, placed herself within the eleven-yard semicircle that surrounded the goal, and prepared for Phil's attack.

Preparation didn't do her much good. Carole admired the way Phil handled his horse with one hand and his racquet with the other, easily dribbling the ball down the field, dodging the ineffectual efforts of her teammates to stop his progress. Just before he reached the penalty line, he picked up the ball, bounced it over the line, picked it up again, and tossed it right between the goalposts.

"Score!" Max called out.

Carole was stunned at the speed with which the goal was made. Phil was really good.

"Did you see that?" she asked Stevie before she had a chance to explode. "He's really good—and smooth! I can't wait to have a chance to try to do what he was doing. I like that technique!"

Stevie glared at her. "If we don't ever get the ball away from them, none of us will ever have a chance to try their techniques, much less hope to score!"

"Begin play!" Max called out to his riders. The Saddle Club returned to the middle of the field to try again.

This time, Phil got the ball on the toss-in. Carole attacked him immediately, head-on, swiped her stick upward, and the ball went careening out of his racquet. Carole was really pleased with herself. That was *good* technique.

"Way to go!" Lisa called over to her. With that, the ball landed on the ground near Lisa. She leaned down to pick it up, but not before the other team's Defense swooped across the field, scooped up the ball, and tossed it to Phil, who caught it in his racquet.

Things went downhill from there. By the end of the six-minute chukka, The Saddle Club girls had committed four more fouls (three of which resulted in goals for Phil's team), three tactical errors (like throwing it through the wrong goal), and innumerable misses, near-misses, and just plain dumb mistakes.

"End of the chukka. Score: Cross County 9, Horse Wise 0."

Stevie groaned.

"Think of it this way, Stevie," Carole said, trying to

console her. "Because it's our first game, we're just playing four chukkas. We've finished one and it's nine to
nothing. So, probably the worst it can be when we're
done is thirty-six–zip. If we were going to play six
chukkas—why, they could run the score up to fifty-four!"

"Shut up," Stevie said. There was murder in her eyes.
Carole took her advice.

The second chukka, played by the B teams, wasn't
quite as bad. Horse Wise actually scored a goal, though it
was because the ball bounced off the Cross County Center's racquet and traveled between the goal posts. The
score at the end of the second chukka was 16–1.

"Let's go for it!" Lisa said eagerly, trying to inspire her
A teammates as they returned to the field.

Stevie glared at her.

Carole would have given Lisa support, but someone
caught her eye. Marie Dana and her mother were standing
by the fence at the edge of the field. Could it be possible
that she'd decided to try riding? Or were they just curious
as they passed by? Perhaps Marie had been enticed by the
showy riding Carole had done in her backyard.

Carole didn't know which it was and it didn't matter.
The fact was that Marie was there. That was enough to
inspire Carole.

"Stand back, world!" Carole announced, bounding
onto the playing field.

"Begin play!" Max called out, tossing the ball to the
players.

The third chukka wasn't as bad as the first two, but it wasn't good enough for Horse Wise to make any progress in scoring. They did make a little bit of progress in defense. Carole actually stopped two almost-certain goal shots and she was able to toss the ball more or less in the direction of her teammates. Her teammates were more or less able to track down her throws successfully and even managed to pass the ball between themselves a few times, though not as many times as the Cross County players. They managed to do it more often and better. They even managed to score, six times.

"Twenty-two to one!" Max announced at the end of the chukka.

"Gee, next time, maybe we should opt for four-minute chukkas," Stevie said angrily.

Carole barely heard her. As she rode toward the edge of the playing field, she saw that Marie was walking away—headed for her car. Carole couldn't let her just leave. She had to talk to her!

Carole handed Starlight's reins to one surprised Pony Clubber and ran after Marie.

"Hey, don't go!" Carole called to her. "Wait! I want to talk to you!"

Mrs. Dana paused and waved to Carole. Marie didn't turn around. She just moved slowly, awkwardly, toward her car.

6

"IT's OKAY," CAROLE said, catching up to Marie. "I know how bad we were. You don't need to be embarrassed by it. You won't have to say anything nice to me about our play—not even the goal I made for the other team."

Marie laughed in spite of herself. "It's not that," she said.

"I was joking," Carole said. "That's the first time we ever played the game. It won't be so awful next time."

There was a twinkle in Marie's eyes. "If they've agreed to play with you again, it must be to bolster their confidence. I can see their schedule now: Lose one. Play one against Horse Wise. Lose one. Play one against Horse Wise."

"Very funny," Carole said. And it *was* kind of funny.

"But the good news is that you're here. Are you going to take lessons? Let me introduce you to Max . . ."

Marie seemed uncomfortable then—as if she wasn't ready to talk or decide. "We were just passing by," she began. "Mom saw you guys riding. I thought it would be okay if we watched. That's all." She turned to finish her walk toward the car.

"But that means you haven't paid the entry fee yet, then, have you?"

"Entry fee?" Marie asked. "You mean there was a charge for watching *that* game?"

"Well, sure," Carole told her. "The charge is that all curious onlookers have to have the grand tour of the whole stable. You've got time now, don't you?"

For a second, Marie just stared at Carole.

"All right. You win," Marie said. "But I'm a really slow walker these days. This could take a while and I might get tired."

The last thing Carole wanted was to have Marie decide she was too tired to finish the grand tour. Then Carole realized she could kill two birds with one stone. She could make sure Marie wouldn't get tired, and she could tempt her with some horseback-riding experience. "You know, we don't have any wheelchairs around here, but we do have a way of getting people around without walking. Why don't you wait here for just a few minutes . . ."

Carole was gone before Marie could protest or change her mind. First, Carole fetched Starlight to park him in his stall until she could untack him. Then, she had a brief word with Max, who agreed with her plan, only because he trusted her judgment, he told her. Then she found Lisa, enlisted her help, and put her plan in action. Then minutes after she'd left Marie, she and Lisa returned, leading Nickel. Nickel was one of Pine Hollow's ponies. He was small enough to be easy to mount, even for somebody with weak legs, and he was gentle enough for anybody to ride, even somebody who wouldn't be able to control him well.

"I'd like to introduce you to Pine Hollow's answer to barrier free. His name is Nickel."

The steel-gray pony looked curiously at Marie. Carole gave Marie a carrot to give to Nickel.

"It's a good way to break the ice," she explained. Then she showed her how to feed it to Nickel. "Put the carrot on your hand and hold it out to him with your fingers flat. You don't want a horse to mistake a finger for a tasty bit of carrot."

Marie followed Carole's instructions. Nickel glanced at the offered hand and sniffed. Then, he picked up the carrot with his soft lips and munched. The smile on Marie's face told Carole everything she needed to know. She might have been part of a miserable loss in polocrosse that day, but everybody was going to win this tougher—and much more important—challenge.

54

"Ready?" Carole asked. Marie nodded. Together, with the help of Lisa and the guidance of Mrs. Dana, they got Marie into Nickel's saddle. It took a while to adjust the stirrups to a level that was comfortable, but Carole was patient and Marie was willing to have the fuss made. Carole sensed that Marie was just plain enjoying being on horseback and that's what this was really all about.

Then, as they were about to begin the tour, Carole saw her father and heard him call her. The tone in his voice wasn't happy. As soon as he spotted her, her marched toward her in his most military Marine Corps stride.

"Can you explain why it is I just saw your horse in his stall with all his tack on fully fifteen minutes after the end of the game?" he demanded.

Colonel Hanson was one of the Horse Wise parent volunteers. He took the job seriously and he was willing to help the riders learn—even when it meant speaking sharply to his daughter. There was a reason she'd left Starlight tacked up and Carole was about to explain it to her father. First, though, she introduced him to Marie. As she introduced him to Mrs. Dana, Carole remembered how interested he'd been to learn about the woman when they were at the hospital.

Carole then explained about showing Marie around, and that the tour included an untacking demonstration at Starlight's stall.

"Okay, okay," Colonel Hanson said. "Go on ahead. I'll

show Mrs. Dana some things, too." He offered Marie's mother his arm gallantly. She took it.

"Please, call me Olivia."

"And I'm Mitch," he said. Off they went.

Carole, Lisa, and Marie headed for the stable. Their first stop was Starlight's stall.

"It's not that leaving his tack on is harmful so much as it's not really fair," Carole explained as she removed the saddle. "I had loosened the girth so he wasn't uncomfortable. Still, his work is over and he deserves a real rest."

"Do you have to do all this work just because you own the horse?" Marie asked.

Carole and Lisa laughed.

"No," Lisa answered. "All riders at Pine Hollow have to take care of the horses they use," she explained. "There are two main reasons. First of all, if the riders pitch in, Max doesn't have to hire so many stablehands and he can keep the costs down. A lot of us couldn't take lessons or belong to Horse Wise if our parents had to pay any more than they do."

"The other reason," Carole continued for Lisa, "is that Max believes horseback riding doesn't begin when you climb in the saddle and finish when you dismount. Horseback riding is really horse care and stable management, too. As far as he's concerned, you aren't learning to ride a horse if all you're ever doing is riding. You need to understand much more about the horse than that.

And the more you know about your horse when you're out of the saddle, the better off you'll both be when you're in it. See?"

"I do see," Marie said. "And you really like to do all this stuff?" she asked, watching as Carole cleaned out some accumulated manure.

"Well . . ." Carole relented. "There are some things I like to do better than others!"

"Don't worry," Lisa said. "That stuff doesn't take much time. The thing that I keep in mind is that it's all about horses. Come on, while Carole finishes up. All she has left to do now is get fresh water and hay for Starlight. I'll introduce you to some of our other horses."

Lisa took the lead rope and walked Nickel slowly along the aisle of the stable.

"This is Topside," she began. "Our friend Stevie usually rides him, but he's a championship show horse and really too valuable for polocrosse, although she used him in a few practices. She was riding a chestnut named Comanche today. Now, here's Pepper. He's the horse I usually ride. And this is Patch—"

They paused at each stall while Lisa made the introductions. Most of the Horse Wise riders had finished their untacking and grooming. The horses were relaxing, munching contentedly on fresh hay and watching Lisa, Marie, and Nickel as they made their way through the stable.

". . . and this is Garnet. This is another boarder

horse, like Starlight. She belongs to Veronica diAngelo, as you can tell by the initials on her blanket."

"Beautiful!" Marie said.

Garnet stuck her head out over the top of her door. Instinctively, Marie reached out to scratch her forehead and rub her cheek. Garnet nodded affectionately.

"Boy, is she friendly!" Marie said, pleased by the mare's response.

Lisa tried to think how to describe the situation. Veronica diAngelo was a spoiled rich girl who had found more ways to get other people to do her work than Lisa would have thought possible. It was hard to imagine ignoring the needs of a beautiful, valuable horse like Garnet, but Veronica managed it. "She is friendly, but it's more like the horse is starved for love," Lisa explained. "Her owner thinks of her as a fashion accessory."

"Oh," Marie said. "How awful."

They met up with Carole in the tack room. Carole and Lisa then pointed out the riders' locker area, Mrs. Reg's office, the feed room, and the indoor ring. "We only ride in there when it's really cold or raining. Outdoors is nicer," Lisa explained.

"You can say that again," Marie said. "I've hardly been allowed to be outdoors for the last few months. I was surprised at how much I missed it."

"Well," Carole continued, "outdoors, we've got the schooling ring, the game field, where today's polocrosse—uh, um—" she couldn't think of the right word. "Game" seemed much too tame.

"Debacle?" Lisa suggested.

"Maybe," Carole said. She turned to Marie. "Lisa is a straight-A student," she explained. "Sometimes she likes to use twenty-five-cent words. Anyway, if *debacle* means 'humiliating defeat,' then it's the right word."

"That's what it means," Lisa said. "And Marie can note, for the record, that sometimes you use Marine Corps terms—like 'humiliating defeat.'"

Carole pretended to be insulted by the dig. "Why, how could you? The Marine Corps never uses the term 'humiliating defeat'—unless, of course, they are talking about something other than the Marine Corps. 'Retreat,' maybe. 'Advancing to the rear,' more likely."

They were still discussing terms like *rout*, *Waterloo*, *drubbing*, *licking*, and *thrashing* when the tour group arrived at the scene of the crime.

It was nearly abandoned now. All the Cross County riders had loaded their horses onto their vans and gone home to celebrate. The Horse Wise Pony Clubbers had dispersed as quickly, but without anything to celebrate. Max and the parent volunteers were having a meeting. The only sight on the playing field was Stevie Lake and Comanche. They were practicing polocrosse.

Using her racquet, Stevie tossed the ball into midfield. Then, she kicked Comanche into a fast canter and approached the ball, trying to pick it up as she whizzed past it. She swung hard at it—and missed. She rode well past the ball, then turned Comanche around and tried it again. She rode even faster. Comanche did just what Stevie told him to do, and Stevie did the best she knew how, but it wasn't good enough. This time, although she was able to touch the ball with her racquet, she still didn't manage to pick it up.

She pulled her horse to a halt, as if she were punishing him. She was too far away for Lisa, Carole, and Marie to hear what she was saying and it was clear Stevie had no idea that anybody was watching her. In fact, Carole suspected that if they'd stood right in front of Stevie and waved, Stevie wouldn't have seen them. Stevie always had the ability to concentrate on a project when she set her mind to it, but Carole and Lisa had never seen her as driven as she was about polocrosse.

Once again, Comanche started cantering toward the ball. Stevie used her polocrosse racquet as a whip and his canter switched to a gallop. Stevie leaned forward then and swung the racquet back for momentum. The horse raced across the field, closing the gap between himself and the ball at a dizzying rate. Now they were almost there.

Stevie began her swing, but seemed to realize in the middle of it that Comanche was too far to the left. She tried to steer him to the right. He was going too fast to make it. Stevie had to make up the difference. She leaned and stretched. She couldn't reach it! She shifted her weight in the saddle, struggling to gain another inch or two toward the right, toward the ball, angling the racquet to be able to scoop it up.

Carole, Lisa, and Marie watched in horror as the scene played itself out. Stevie leaned to the right even more, putting all her weight on her right stirrup, straining and extending herself beyond the limits of her own balance. Then, as if in slow motion, Stevie's friends saw Stevie's left leg rise up over the far side of the horse, free of its stirrup, and Stevie herself flew out of Comanche's saddle. She landed on top of the polocrosse ball. Comanche kept on going.

It was almost comical. But Carole knew right away that it wasn't comical. The shriek that came from Stevie wasn't frustration and wasn't anger. It was pain. She lay in the middle of the field, clutching her ankle.

Stevie was in trouble; Carole and Lisa had to get to her!

7

"STEVIE!" CAROLE AND Lisa called to her.

"Ouch!" Stevie replied. "It's my ankle—and it hurts!"

Lisa got there first. When Carole reached her friends and squatted next to where Stevie lay, she knew exactly what had to be done.

"Get her boot off if you can, before the ankle gets so big that the boot has to be cut off," she advised Lisa. Lisa unbuckled Stevie's jodhpur boot immediately and pulled it off gently.

"Ouch!" Stevie said again. "But thanks." Tears welled in her eyes. Carole knew her pain was real.

"I'll get help," Carole said. She stood up to run to the stable and saw that she didn't have to. For there, riding as fast as she could toward the stable, was Marie.

"Mom! Come out here. There's been an accident!"

As soon as Max and some of the Horse Wise parent volunteers came out the door of the stable, Marie turned Nickel around and kicked him into a canter to take her into the field.

She rode easily and surely, rocking with the horse's motion. As she neared the place where Stevie lay, she drew Nickel to a halt. He stopped immediately.

"Nice riding!" Stevie said, genuinely impressed. Carole was impressed, too, but at the moment, she was happy that Stevie had something to take her mind off her pain.

Very soon after that, Max and Mrs. Dana reached Stevie. Max took one look at her ankle, now enormously swollen, and said, "Hospital."

For a few minutes, there was discussion about who should take her. In the end, Mrs. Dana won the privilege because her car was set up for use by an injured person. There were a lot of cushions, and a space to lie down.

Colonel Hanson climbed into the front seat next to Mrs. Dana, telling Carole to have Mrs. Reg call Stevie's parents, and they left.

The last thing Carole saw as the car pulled out of the driveway was Stevie, sitting up in the backseat. She was trying hard to smile, but the tears were running down her cheeks. It really hurt.

"Oh!" Carole said almost involuntarily, feeling the pain for her friend.

"She's going to be okay," Marie said reassuringly.

"They're good over at that emergency room. They'll take care of her."

"Besides," Lisa reminded Carole, "just a few weeks ago, Stevie was in charge of a whole day of entertainment for the patients there. They love her and won't let anything happen to her!"

Carole tried to smile, but, like Stevie, she felt the pain anyway. Injuries, hospitals, emergencies—no matter what, they always made her think of all the time her mother had spent in the hospital. She suspected that some of the same thoughts were running through Marie's head. Then she knew it was time to do something more constructive.

"I think we ought to round up Comanche. Where has he gotten to?"

She looked around. The horse was at the far end of the playing field, munching on some strands of grass. Carole whistled hopefully. He glanced at her and then apparently decided he wasn't interested. He continued munching.

She and Lisa began to walk toward him. He walked away from them. It seemed that he'd been upset by the accident and wasn't quite ready to return to his stall. Every time they approached him, he moved away, each time getting farther from the corner of the field, farther from the fence, and harder to catch.

Carole was frustrated. Normally, she had all the time in the world for a horse, no matter what kind of mood he was in. But Comanche's misbehaving didn't suit her at all. Carole wasn't quite sure what to do. If she'd been on horseback, it just would have been a matter of outsmarting Comanche. On foot, however, they had to outrun *and* outsmart, and Comanche was just plain faster than they were.

Then, without warning, Marie came to their rescue. She'd circled around behind Comanche when his attention was on Carole and Lisa and, like a cowboy rounding up a stray, she moved him ahead by clapping him on the rump. He was startled and began trotting forward— straight toward Lisa and Carole.

He tried to dodge, but it didn't do him any good. He ended up loping between Lisa and Carole, enabling them each to grab onto his reins. His rebellion was over.

"There boy, there. It's okay," Carole said as soothingly as she could. His eyes were opened wide, his ears flattened. She patted him on the neck, speaking in a low, steady voice all the time. "We're here with you. Nobody's mad at you. You were doing what Stevie told you. No problem, boy. It's okay." Carole rubbed his cheek. He relaxed then, his eyes narrowed, and his ears popped up again. He pranced nervously, but he was under control.

Carole checked that the tack hadn't gotten disarrayed in the accident and, finding it secure, she mounted the horse. As soon as she sat in his saddle and took firm control of his reins, he calmed down. It took a few tries to get him walking toward the stable, but by the time he reached the schooling ring, he was his old well-behaved self.

Carole dismounted, walked Comanche to his stall, removed his tack, and slid the door closed. Then she turned to Marie, who, along with Lisa, had followed her into the stable.

"Like Stevie said earlier, that was some riding. You are really good! You told me you'd just done a little, but you really know what you're doing."

"No," Marie protested. "I just saw a chance and thought maybe—"

"Nonsense," Lisa said in her matter-of-fact way. "You knew exactly what you were doing, and you were terrific at it. We all owe you thanks."

It was so clearly true that Marie didn't try to deny it. The girl was obviously a good rider with some experience.

"Come on, let's finish up and get over to the hospital. I want to see what kind of mischief Stevie is really up to!"

Lisa and Carole helped Marie dismount and then they untacked and groomed Nickel. Carole saw to it he got an extra-special ration of oats for his good partnership with Marie.

Since Marie's legs were still weak, and since they'd been used so much that day, Carole suggested that Marie might just want to sit down in Max's office and not walk to the hospital. Marie wouldn't hear of it. She insisted on accompanying them, and both Carole and Lisa thought she was a welcome companion.

When the girls got to the hospital, they peered through a small window into the emergency room and saw a flurry of activity around one particular patient: Stevie Lake.

"Oh, no, what could be going on in there?" Carole moaned.

"I don't know," Lisa said.

"Let me see," Marie said, looking in with them.

Then, when the door opened, their question was answered, for they heard Stevie's unmistakable voice saying, "What's that? I can't hear you, Doc, I've got a banana in my ear!" It was followed by a burst of laughter.

"She's telling jokes!" Carole said. "Old ones! Bad ones—just like the kind my father tells. Here we are, thinking the worst, and Stevie's cracking jokes!"

"I'm afraid Stevie's not the only one," Lisa said ominously.

They listened again.

"Okay, so this gorilla goes into a soda shop—"

"Dad!" Carole yowled. She burst through the door, followed by Lisa and Marie.

"Just a second, honey," Colonel Hanson said.

Carole was not going to be stopped. "How's Stevie?" she demanded.

"I'm fine," Stevie said. "Now let your dad finish this one. It's one of my favorites."

Stunned, Carole, Lisa, and Marie waited.

"And the gorilla orders a chocolate sundae. The soda jerk is a little nervous, but he figures he can pull one over on the dumb gorilla. 'That'll be ten dollars,' he tells the gorilla. The gorilla pays him and eats the sundae. 'You know, we don't get many gorillas in here,' the soda jerk says. 'I'm not surprised,' the gorilla tells him. 'With sundaes at ten dollars apiece!'"

"All right. Enough! My turn," Carole interrupted the stand-up routines. "What is the story on Stevie's ankle besides 'fine'? 'Fine' doesn't swell up like a balloon."

Stevie scooted forward on the gurney and showed Carole her ankle. It had a big elastic bandage that came, apparently, accompanied by a pair of crutches.

"It's sprained, not broken," she said. "I have to keep the bandage on and I'm not allowed to walk on it—or ride—for at least three weeks. The good news is that it's not broken. That would be more like six weeks."

"Three weeks without riding?" Carole said. Stevie nodded. "But aren't we supposed to have another polocrosse match with Cross County in two weeks?" Carole asked. Nobody who knew Carole was surprised at her reaction. To her, walking was simply not as important as riding.

Stifling a smile, Lisa nudged her. "Look at the bright side of that," she said. "We can forfeit this time instead of being massacred!"

"Oh, no!" Stevie said. "We'll play again. It's just that

this time, I'll coach, not ride. I did learn a lot about the sport this afternoon."

"Right," a doctor piped in. "Like the fastest route to the emergency room!" Everybody, except Carole and Lisa, laughed.

Stevie's father then offered his daughter a hand to help her get down from the gurney. "I think it's time to go," he said. "After all, I'm sure these people have a lot of things to do besides swapping jokes with you!"

A few of the doctors and nurses tried to convince Mr. Lake that they'd really rather tell jokes, but when the P.A. announced that an ambulance was arriving, they were all business. They barely paused to wave good-bye as Stevie hobbled out, trailed by her friends, her father, Colonel Hanson, Max, Mrs. Dana, and Marie.

Stevie accepted some help from her father and from Colonel Hanson. Max walked between Marie and her mother. He offered his arm to Marie for any extra help she might need.

"We need to talk," he said to her.

"We do?" Marie asked. "Did I do something wrong?"

"Not at all," he said. "In fact, you did something very right. You did a good job of riding and it helped Stevie tremendously."

"Uh, Max," Carole said. "You should have seen what she did when Lisa and I were trying to round up Comanche. You'd think she was a natural-born cowpoke.

She flushed him right away from the fence and into our waiting arms. This girl is good!"

"Here, here," Lisa added.

"And she's going to get better," Max said.

Marie looked at her mother's worried face. "I was all for it before today, but now I see it can be quite dangerous," Mrs. Dana said.

"Hey, I've been riding for years," Stevie said. "This is the first time I ever got hurt—oh, yeah, except for the poison ivy I got when I fell off Patch, and the time I bruised my shoulder . . ."

"Shut up, Stevie," Carole said.

"Uh, Stevie is a somewhat rambunctious rider," Max explained. "Carole sets a better example."

"Marie doesn't have to do anything wild or dangerous," Carole said. "She'll be safe as can be. We'll take care of her."

Marie looked at Carole and then back at Max. "Is this some sort of conspiracy?" she asked.

"It'll be for your own good, Marie," Carole said. "You told me your physical therapist wants you to ride."

"It'll strengthen those weak legs," Lisa added.

"But most of all, it'll be fun," Carole said. "That's what riding is—fun."

"Most of the time," Stevie said. "As long as you're careful."

"All right, all right. I give in. I'll ride. When's my first lesson?"

"Monday, after school?" Max suggested. "We'll have one session for just the two of us and then, if I think you're up for it, you can join the class on Tuesday—if your mother approves." He looked to her for assent.

"Oh, I don't know," Mrs. Dana said. "I just worry that—"

Carole's father came to the rescue. "You don't have to worry about her, Olivia. Max is the best instructor there is. And once she's in the class, this threesome will see to it she's safe."

"Okay. You can try it," she agreed finally.

"Monday at three-thirty," Marie said.

Carole sighed with relief. Her friends had helped her achieve her goal. And if they could talk Marie Dana's mother into letting Marie take riding lessons, they could do anything, couldn't they?

8

"THE SADDLE CLUB shall come to order," Stevie announced. Lisa and Carole both looked at her in surprise. Saddle Club meetings usually just took place wherever and whenever anybody thought they were having a Saddle Club meeting. Except for once a long time ago, when Lisa thought having rules was a good idea, nobody called them to order and nobody adjourned them. However, this time, things were a little different.

The three girls were at Stevie's house. They were supposed to be having a sleepover at Lisa's house, but since the events of the day had included Stevie's sprained ankle, her parents thought she should be at home. She'd talked them into letting Carole and Lisa stay over with her.

What made it different from other sleepovers was all

the attention Stevie was getting from her family. Her father had stopped by her bedroom twice to see if she wanted anything. Her brother Chad had brought all the couch pillows from the den and made a sort of throne for her on her bed. Lisa suspected that was why she sounded like a queen when she announced the beginning of the meeting.

Alex, Stevie's twin brother, had knocked on the door three times to ask if there was anything Stevie wanted. She had been able to think of things he could do for her and her friends. She got away with the round of sodas and one tray of cookies and milk. He hadn't been quite so gracious with the second tray of cookies and Lisa suspected they wouldn't be seeing him again for a while.

On the other hand, Michael, Stevie's younger brother, had been talked into paying a quarter just to see how swollen the ankle was.

"Oh, gross!" he'd declared gleefully and then headed for the phone.

"I think he's calling up all his friends now," Stevie said. "My guess is he's going to charge them fifty cents—and pay me half of it. It's good business, you know."

"Like brother, like sister," Lisa had said in total amazement.

Carole had just laughed.

"Okay, so we've come to order," Lisa said. "What's our first order of business?"

"To talk about today's polocrosse match," Stevie said.

"If you weren't sitting on all of the pillows, I'd throw one at you," Carole told her. "There's only one word for the game today and that's 'embarrassing.'"

"Agreed. Now let's talk about the next match in two weeks."

"We can't play," Lisa said. "As I told you, we're short a player now. We can't have just five on the team."

"What about Marie?" Stevie asked. "Is she as good as you guys say she is?"

Carole thought about that. It wasn't an easy question. Marie had shown them some pretty good riding, she pointed out, but it might just have been luck. Maybe she was only good in the clutch.

"Then she'll be *great* at polocrosse!" Stevie said excitedly.

Lisa shook her head. "She could be, but I have the feeling that, in the long run, Marie might not be the biggest problem there. I think it's her mother, don't you, Carole?"

"Yes. I know the symptoms, too. Although it's been two years since my mother died, my father sometimes suffers from the same thing. It's overconcern. If I sneeze, he's convinced I've got a cold, if I blow my nose, it's the flu. And then, if he hears me cough, it's pneumonia."

"I never noticed that about him," Stevie said.

"Most of the time he's pretty relaxed and then sometimes, for no reason I can figure out, all of a sudden he can't stop worrying about me. I can't predict it. I can't prevent it. The other day, for instance, he made me take my temperature four times and I was perfectly healthy.

"In Marie's case, it's a little easier to understand. Her father just died a few months ago. It was in an accident and her mother may be worried she'll lose Marie." Carole paused and looked at her friends. "Does this make me sound like a cut-rate psychiatrist?" she joked.

"No," Lisa said. "It makes you sound like you know what you're talking about."

"So, what do you do about your father?" Stevie asked.

"Most of the time, I don't have to do anything," Carole said. "After a few days, my father comes to his senses, or he gets tired of reading 98.6°, or he gets distracted by some Marine Corps crisis or something else. The fastest cure is definitely distraction."

Stevie picked up an oatmeal cookie and munched on it thoughtfully. "Hmmmm," she said.

"The wheels are turning," Lisa said. "I can see it. She's got that look."

Carole always felt an odd mixture of curiosity and concern when Stevie got that look. She knew her friend was scheming and Stevie's schemes were always interesting. Sometimes, though, they were trouble.

"What are you thinking about?" she asked. She couldn't wait for the answer.

"Oh, distractions, of course," Stevie said airily. "Now, what's the most obvious distraction for a woman? A man," she said, answering her own question. "I know her husband just died and she's probably not really interested in dating or anything, but everybody can use a friend, right?"

"Sure," Lisa said. "But just who do you have in mind to match up with Marie's mother? Max?"

"Max! Are you crazy? No, of course not. I was thinking more along the lines of everybody's favorite Marine Corps colonel."

"Dad?"

"You have another favorite colonel?"

"No, it's just—"

"Has he got a new girlfriend?" Stevie asked.

"Nothing serious," Carole said. "There's a woman he plays cards with sometimes and somebody else he plays tennis with, but I'm not aware of any serious dating going on. Let me think a minute about this, okay?"

"Sure," Stevie agreed readily. "After all, it's your dad's future we're talking about here."

That time, Carole did find a pillow to toss at Stevie. Then, while Stevie moaned and groaned and acted as if the gently tossed pillow had caused her agonizing pain, Carole thought.

She recalled that her father had asked about Mrs. Dana the first time he'd seen her. She recalled their first meeting at Pine Hollow—the sweet "Call me Olivia," "And I'm Mitch," exchange. She recalled how her father had hopped into the car with Mrs. Dana to take Stevie to the hospital.

"So?" Stevie asked expectantly.

"So, I suspect that you wouldn't get a lot of resistance from my dad, though I don't recommend that we go about this directly. I mean, if we tell him we want him to like Mrs. Dana—"

"Don't be silly," Stevie said. "I was planning to be much more subtle than that."

"Such as?" Lisa asked.

"Such as," Stevie said, turning to Carole, "why don't you make sure your father comes to pick you up early on Tuesday. You could, for instance, forget there is polocrosse practice after class. We know Mrs. Dana will be there for class. As long as Marie sticks around to watch practice, the two of them will have at least an hour together. We can just let nature take its course."

"Brilliant," Lisa said.

"Elementary," Stevie said.

"Scary," concluded Carole.

"Yeah," said Stevie. "What if it turns out that Marie doesn't want to play polocrosse—or if she's no good at it?"

Carole tossed another pillow at her.

Then the phone rang. Stevie answered it and Carole and Lisa could tell by her tone of voice that it was Phil calling. When the two of them were on opposite teams in the field, Stevie was all competition. When they were on opposite ends of the telephone, it was usually quite a different thing.

"Oh, hi!" Steve greeted him. "Wait until I tell you what happened after you guys left," she began, relating the story of her ankle.

Carole and Lisa knew they had a lot to talk about. Lisa tugged on Carole's sleeve and the two of them tiptoed out of Stevie's room. They went down to the kitchen, where Mrs. Lake had left a bowl of red grapes for them. They were a welcome change from all the cookies Alex had delivered to Stevie's room.

"We have another problem, you know," Carole said, tossing one grape up and catching it in her mouth.

"What's that?" Lisa asked. She tried the tossing trick. It didn't work. She retrieved the grape, threw it out, and resumed eating grapes in the more usual manner.

"Is Stevie going to be any better as a nonriding coach than she was a riding one? I mean, none of us can take any more of her yelling and screaming. But when she gets that competitive bee in her bonnet—"

"She's as much fun to be with as an entire hive of bees," Lisa finished the thought. "Maybe we'd better see how things are going up there," Lisa suggested. "She sounded all sweetness and light when she got on the phone, but I have the feeling that as this conversation goes, so go our practices for the next two weeks!"

"Let's go," Carole agreed. The girls clipped off some of the grapes, put them on a plate, and took them back up to Stevie's room.

"Oh, no, it doesn't hurt *too* much," Stevie was saying

into the phone. "And besides, Carole and Lisa are here. They're really taking care of me. . . . Of course I'm disappointed I won't be able to play in the next game, but believe me, I'll be there cheering for the best team. . . . No, that's not exactly what I meant, Phil. . . . Well, you'll see. Anyway, thanks for calling. I'll talk to you in a couple of days. Bye!"

She cradled the phone and turned to her friends. "Can you believe it?" she asked. "He still thinks his team can beat ours!"

Lisa sat down on the bed and gave Stevie her most serious straight-A-student look. "Stevie, we've got to talk," she began.

CAROLE COULDN'T HELP herself. She was supposed to be saddling Starlight to take him out for a ride, but something more interesting was going on in the ring next to his stall. Marie was having her first riding lesson at Pine Hollow.

Carole had been in the tack room when Marie arrived, accompanied by both her mother and her physical therapist. She'd kept out of sight, but she hadn't missed a thing. Mrs. Dana was afraid that Marie would get hurt. The physical therapist kept talking about muscle groups. Max and Marie stuck to a more interesting subject: horses.

Marie told Max that she had taken lessons for two years before she and her parents had moved to Willow Creek a year ago.

"I'm an intermediate rider," she said. "At least I was."

"Well, then, you will be again," he said. "Now let's get you up here."

He boosted her into the saddle. This time, she was riding Patch, a gentle, reliable horse. Max checked the way she held the reins, and she was doing it right. He told Marie to grip firmly with her legs. The therapist beamed. Patch began to walk.

At Max's insistence, Mrs. Dana and the therapist retreated to a bench on the side of the ring. Mrs. Dana's right hand went automatically to her mouth as she began chewing on her nails. The therapist picked up a pencil and began making notes on a clipboard.

Much more interesting to Carole, however, was what was happening in the ring. Max was being himself, a strict instructor. Patch was acting as he always did. The interesting part was what was happening to Marie.

When she'd first climbed into the saddle, fear had shown in her face. She followed instructions, gripping with her legs and moving the horse forward. Max had her ride him through a circle and then a figure eight at a walk. Each time the horse responded to an order Marie gave him, she grinned. Carole thought she knew exactly how Marie was feeling. It was the same way she felt every time she got on a horse, and it was a feeling she never tired of.

Marie had spent months immobilized and lying flat in bed, and a lot of time since then doing everything her mother or therapist told her. Her very life had been controlled by pain and discomfort and by her grief at her father's death. She'd had no say in anything that had happened to her for a very long time. Now, in the saddle on Patch's back, she was in charge. Patch, a very large animal, was doing exactly what she told him to do. And most important, it was fun.

"Okay?" Max asked, though Carole was sure he knew the answer.

"I'm fine," Marie said quietly. "We're fine." She leaned forward and patted Patch's neck. That was just what Carole would have done then, too.

The therapist interrupted with something about muscle groups and stretching. Max reminded Marie about riding in the two-point—or jump—position, meaning she was to let all of her weight sink into her heels, rise out of the seat, flex her knees, keep her back completely straight, and rest her hands on the horse's neck for balance. The therapist nodded sagely. Mrs. Dana switched to biting the nails of her left hand, and Max said "Good." Marie beamed.

So did Carole. She knew then that Marie would be in her class on Tuesday, at Horse Wise on Saturday and, with a bit of luck in the "distraction" department, that she would join the polocrosse team. Satisfied with what she'd seen, she returned her attention to Starlight. It was time for him to get some exercise.

"NEED SOME HELP with the saddle?" Lisa asked Marie on Tuesday afternoon before riding class.

"Just if you could watch and see if I'm doing it right," Marie said. "It's been a long time."

Lisa watched. Marie took a bit longer than the others but she did just fine. Lisa had to pitch in a little to remind her about the buckles on the bridle, but it was obvious that Marie was eager to do it right. She'd learn without any trouble. And she seemed barely to notice her pain.

Lisa had tied Pepper up near the entrance to the outdoor ring where class would take place. She helped Marie mount Patch and led the horse through the aisles of the stable.

"First things first," she said. "And the first thing you need to do when you ride at Pine Hollow is to touch the good-luck horseshoe." She pointed to the horseshoe nailed by the doorway. Marie touched it as instructed. "No Pine Hollow rider has ever been seriously hurt—and remember, Stevie's injury wasn't serious—if she touches this first." In spite of her assurances to Marie, she made a note to ask Stevie if, by chance, she'd forgotten to touch the horseshoe on Saturday.

There were three spectators for the class. Stevie was there, watching, and obviously wishing she could be on a horse. Her swollen leg was still securely bandaged and her crutches were very much in evidence. In fact, Stevie seemed to be mastering the art of scooting faster than a speeding bullet with her crutches. Lisa hoped she wouldn't hurt herself worse that way!

The other two spectators were Marie's mother and her physical therapist. They leaned forward eagerly at the rail. Her mother appeared worried. The physical therapist was taking notes on her clipboard.

Class began. First, Max introduced Marie to the other riders. Then he began the instruction by working on gaits. They practiced changing gaits mostly between walking and trotting. Lisa suspected Max was taking it a little easy on the whole class because of Marie. Nobody else seemed to notice, though, and everybody benefited from the practice.

Max then had the whole class go through a series of leg-strengthening exercises. Again, Lisa thought these were primarily for Marie's benefit. She could feel her own muscles responding to the activities and suspected they would help all of the students.

It was time then for a game, and the bright spring afternoon sun suggested shadow tag. Lisa glanced at Stevie. The sidelined girl's face fell. Shadow tag was one of her favorites. She was really good at it.

"You're It!" Max announced, pointing to Lisa.

The game was on. This wasn't Lisa's favorite game. She hated being It. She wanted to tag somebody as quickly as possible and then try to stay out of everybody's way. She looked around. Marie wasn't far from her. The temptation was great. After all, Marie was new at the game, new at Pine Hollow. She ought to be an easy target in shadow tag.

Lisa and Pepper lunged at Marie's shadow. Marie saw the attack coming. She checked her own shadow, judged Lisa's distance, and did the only thing she could. She shifted her direction, forcing Lisa and Pepper to pass on her nonshadow side.

Lisa groaned in frustration. The rest of the riders applauded Marie's clever move.

"Nice going," Max said. Even Lisa was impressed.

Eventually Lisa tagged Adam, who tagged Betsy, who tagged Polly, who caught Carole off guard, and she tried, once again, to tag Marie.

Carole began to approach Marie from behind, but she hadn't fooled Marie at all. Marie and Patch took off for the far end of the ring. Carole pursued them. Marie turned Patch to the right and circled back, cleverly keeping her shadow on the edge of the ring, almost impossible to reach. Nevertheless, Carole continued the pursuit. For a minute, it looked as if Carole would have Marie cornered, but Marie got Patch to dodge away, evading what seemed like an inevitable tag.

Carole gave up. Since all the other riders were just standing still watching the Carole and Marie Show, it was easy for Carole to tag Adam. He accepted the tag with good grace, but informed Carole immediately that he was smarter than she was because he wasn't going to try to go after Marie, who was obviously better at this game than any of them. He was going to go after . . .

"Lisa! You're It!" he announced.

A few minutes later, with Lisa still It, the game ended. Max called them to order and told them to pair up for the final exercise.

"You mean class is almost over?" Marie asked.

"Yes, it's been an hour," Max told her.

It was clear Marie couldn't believe it. Lisa was really happy to know she'd had so much fun that the time had flown for her, as it always did for The Saddle Club.

Max lined them up and had them parade around the ring, once again going through their gait changes, this time keeping pace with their partners. Finally, it was time for somebody to pick the soda whip—Max's way of designating one rider to bring a drink to all of the others—and the horses drew to the side of the ring for dismounting. Class was done.

From the edge of the ring, Stevie announced that polocrosse practice would begin in fifteen minutes for all members of the Horse Wise polocrosse team. Those who weren't participating were invited to watch.

Of course, she meant Marie.

Max and the therapist were helping Marie get down from Patch's saddle. "I'm okay, I'm okay. I can do it myself," she said with a trace of irritation.

Her mother remained concerned. Her therapist just watched proudly. Obviously, she was happy with what was happening to Marie's legs.

"Very good!" a familiar male voice said, admiring Marie's dismount. It was Colonel Hanson. He'd arrived early, just as The Saddle Club had planned. That was Carole's cue, but she was in the stable. Lisa had to get her so she could tell her father she'd forgotten about polocrosse and ask if he would mind waiting.

Lisa shooed Pepper into his stall, tracked down Carole and Starlight, and reminded her about her part in the subterfuge. Stevie's assigned job was to get Marie to stay to watch polocrosse practice.

Lisa followed Carole back out to the ring. They were both pleased to see that they had to interrupt a conversation between Colonel Hanson and Mrs. Dana.

"Oh, Dad, I'm so sorry!" Carole said. "I forgot all about polocrosse practice when I asked you to pick me up today. Would you mind sticking around? It'll only be a half hour or so."

"Wait? Here?" he said. "Well, Marie just told her mother she wants to watch the practice. Why don't Olivia and I take a walk. We'll meet you girls at TD's after practice, okay?"

It was better than they could have imagined. TD's was an ice cream parlor at the nearby shopping center.

"Fine, Dad," Carole said. Then, she touched her own forehead lightly. "You know, Dad, I think I might have a slight fever. Do you want to check it for me?"

Colonel Hanson put the back of his hand on her forehead. "You seem fine to me," he said. Then he offered Mrs. Dana his arm and the two of them walked off to the ice cream parlor together.

"Distraction," Carole said to Lisa. "I told you, it's the best route every time!"

The two of them burst into giggles and ran to find Stevie. They couldn't wait to tell her!

POLOCROSSE PRACTICE, COACHED by Stevie Lake, was unlike any experience the riders had had with polocrosse before. Stevie was a changed person. She was all business, with no yelling, no screaming, no putting down.

She had designed a number of exercises to develop polocrosse skills.

"The game is primarily won with good pickups, passes, and catches. We all already know how to ride a horse. What we need to learn is to handle the racquets and balls. When we can do those things, we can defend, attack, and score. Now, first, pickups."

Stevie had been studying hard and she shared her knowledge well. Still sitting at the edge of the ring, because she couldn't even be on horseback with her sore ankle, she showed how to sweep the racquet just along the surface of the ground to pick up the ball.

"See, if you swat down at it, all you're going to get for your trouble is a racquetful of dirt—if not worse." There were laughs. All the riders practiced leaning forward and sweeping the ground with their racquets. Then Stevie had each of them pick up the ball, first standing still, then walking, then trotting.

"Hey, it gets better!" Lisa declared, proudly showing off the trophy in her racquet's net.

"Not *it*—you," Stevie corrected her. "When you practice, you get better. Next, throwing."

She led them through her program of exercises. With throwing, that included underarm tosses, sidearm tosses, and overhead heaves. Then it was time to practice catching. The riders faced each other on horseback and threw the balls back and forth. At first, catching was a disaster. Polocrosse balls were flying everywhere except into partners' racquets. But then, it changed. By the fourth or fifth attempts, the riders learned how to control their racquets both as throwing and catching instruments. They were a long way from being good, but they were learning and that was something they hadn't done much of in their first week as polocrosse players.

When the half hour was up, all of the riders thought they had done a lot of work and that it had been good work. Everybody wanted to thank Stevie for her coaching. She had run a really good practice.

The riders untacked and groomed their horses, fed them and gave them water, and then changed into street clothes and shoes. Within a very short time, there were only four girls left at Pine Hollow—The Saddle Club and Marie.

"Where's my mother?" Marie asked, suddenly realizing she hadn't seen her since the end of class.

Lisa, Carole, and Stevie looked at one another mischievously.

"I think she got distracted by something," Stevie said, putting a lot of emphasis on the word *distracted*.

"By some*one*," Lisa corrected her friend.

"What are you talking about?" Marie asked.

All eyes turned to Carole. "If you can believe it, my father invited your mother to go with him to the ice cream parlor."

A grin crossed Marie's face. "You know what?" she asked. "That's the first time in almost four months that I haven't known exactly where my mother was. I mean, she didn't even leave an emergency phone number!"

TWO DAYS LATER, Carole was tightening Patch's girth for Marie. She handed the reins to Marie. "Let me just bring Starlight to the doorway and then I'll help you into the saddle," she said.

Marie's eyes were twinkling with excitement. She was obviously eager to get going.

Carole had arranged to take Marie on a trail ride. All she had had to do was promise Max that she would watch her every second and pledge to Mrs. Dana that she wouldn't let Marie's horse go faster than a walk.

Within a few minutes, all the work was done and they were ready to go. Carole led the way to the stable's entrance. They each brushed the good-luck horseshoe and they were off.

The two girls rode through the fields behind Pine Hollow side-by-side. Soon, they were talking easily, as if they had been riding through fields together all their lives.

"This really is wonderful," Marie said. "I spent so many months indoors that I had almost forgotten how nice fresh air is, how wonderful the fields smell in the spring, how beautiful the sky is when it's filled with fluffy clouds, how—oh, I guess I must sound foolish. Is that what you were thinking?" she asked, blushing suddenly.

"Not at all," Carole said. "I was thinking how much you've changed."

"I have?" Marie asked.

"You don't know?" Carole was surprised.

Marie shook her head.

"Well, when I first met you a few weeks ago, you didn't want to talk, much less admit that anything was wrong, or even ask for help. Now, you're having fun, aren't you?"

"Yeah, I am," she said. "And I want to have more fun, too. Can we trot?"

"No way," Carole said. "I promised Max and your mother on a stack of Bibles that this would be the safest trail ride anybody ever took. So, there is nothing you can say to convince me that we ought to go any faster than a very sedate walk"—she paused for effect—"at least as long as we are within sight of Pine Hollow. Come on, follow me."

With that Carole led the way around a small hill and

obscured the stable from their view. "Ready?" she asked. Marie nodded. Carole gave Starlight a little nudge. It didn't take much encouragement. He began trotting right away. As soon as Marie gave Patch the signal, he broke into a trot, too.

Carole let Patch come up beside Starlight so she could watch Marie carefully. As she had seen when the girl was in class, Marie knew what she was doing. She posted with the two-beat gait of Patch's trot, rising slightly and sitting, still keeping her back straight and her hands still.

"Nice," Carole said, genuinely admiring Marie's position. "You do know what you're doing."

Marie just smiled. It wasn't clear to Carole whether that was because she was pleased by Carole's compliment or simply happy to be trotting. It didn't matter. A smile from Marie was a very welcome thing.

Carole drew Starlight back down to a walk. She patted his neck reflexively. It was a way she could always tell him how much she loved riding him. Marie did the same with Patch.

"You're right," Marie said, walking side-by-side with Carole. "I have changed. I'm happy now and I'm beginning to think it's all right to be happy."

"I know. All of a sudden, there comes a time when you realize you don't have to feel guilty about being happy and having fun. That's when you can really start living your life again."

Marie looked at her strangely. "How did you know?"

Carole remembered then that she'd been keeping a secret from Marie. She'd never told her new friend about her own mother's death. At first, it had seemed as if it would be sort of phony to tell her—as if Carole were trying to prove something, or as if she expected Marie to feel sorry for her, too. That wasn't how Carole felt, but she'd been afraid it would be how Marie would react. Now, however, the fact that she hadn't told her made her feel dishonest, as if she'd been withholding something. Carole had to come clean and she wasn't quite sure what to say.

"Well, my mother—"

"Your parents are divorced, aren't they?" Marie asked.

Carole shook her head. "No," she said. There was a long silence. Then she said the words. "My mother died."

"A long time ago?" Marie asked.

"Just two years. Seems like yesterday."

"Why didn't you tell me?"

Why? It sounded so strange even to her that Carole couldn't explain it. Why not?

"I don't know," she began.

"You were holding out on me," Marie said accusingly. "Did you think it was some kind of dirty secret?"

"No," Carole told her. "I guess it seems that way. It's just that—well, I didn't know *how* to tell you."

Carole pulled Starlight to a complete stop. Marie stopped Patch next to her. The two girls stared at each other, looking for clues and answers. Carole wished that she had told Marie when she'd first met her, wished she hadn't kept the secret, which wasn't a secret at all and certainly wasn't a dirty secret. She just hadn't wanted to talk about it and now she had to, but she didn't know what to say.

"It's not fair, you know," Marie said. "Having my father die is bad enough without people trying to lie to me about things. For a long time when I was in the hospital, they lied to me about him. 'He's still sick,' they said. 'He'll come visit you when he can.' Once a nurse even told me he'd been there but that I'd been asleep and they hadn't wanted to wake me up. I knew it was a lie. That was when I knew he was dead."

"I hate lies, you know. I hated it when the doctors told me things wouldn't hurt—and they did. I hated it when they told me I'd be up and walking in no time, and I wasn't. I hated it when they said physical therapy would be easy and fun, but it wasn't either. I hate lies, Carole, and you told me a lie!"

The lines in Marie's face hardened with anger. Carole wanted to speak, wanted to reach out with her heart, but there were no words. Before she could say anything at all, Marie gave Patch a big kick and the two of them bolted off—not at a leisurely walk, but at a trot that rapidly turned into a canter.

When it came to words, Carole could often be tongue-tied, but when the subject was horses, she just about always knew what to do. Marie was a pretty good rider. That was clear to anybody who'd seen her on horseback, but she was also a girl who was still recovering from some serious injuries and she had no business galloping off through the fields. No matter how angry Marie was at Carole, Carole had a responsibility to Marie, to Marie's mother, and to Max. She couldn't let Marie do something recklessly dangerous!

Carole turned Starlight around and bounded after her. Patch was a fine and gentle horse, but he was also a fast horse and once he got an idea about running free, it was sometimes pretty hard to convince him to stop. By the time Carole and Starlight were aimed in Marie's direction, Patch was two hillocks away, and still going strong.

"Go, boy! Go!" Carole said, touching Starlight gently with her riding crop. He got the idea. He instinctively understood what Carole needed. Carole was grateful then for the fact that horses are naturally competitive. They love races and Starlight was no exception. As far as he was concerned, Patch's head start was just all the more reason to go fast.

Carole gripped tightly with her legs and they flew after Marie and Patch. As they got closer, she was afraid that Marie was struggling with Patch. Riding a horse under control wasn't always easy, even with strong legs. Riding a horse out of control was hard, even for an experienced rider, and nearly impossible for somebody with weak legs.

"Help!" Marie shrieked. She was doing the best she

could but it was just too much for her. Her arms flailed over her head and the reins flew out of her hands.

"Grab his mane!" Carole yelled.

Marie's fingers clutched at Patch's mane.

Carole focused every bit of her concentration on reaching Patch and grabbing the loose reins. Every time her concentration slipped the least bit, her mind filled with a terrible image of Marie falling on the ground and hurting herself. If Marie had to go back to the hospital now, Carole didn't know how she'd ever forgive herself—and she was sure Marie would never forgive her.

"Hold with your legs! I'm almost there," Carole called out. She tried to mask the fear in her voice. She was sure it wouldn't do Marie any good to think that she was scared, too.

Then, a funny thing happened. Starlight pulled up to Patch and the two of them ran neck and neck together. Carole tried to reach over to grab Patch's reins. Before she could get them, however, Patch slowed down and drew to a halt. As far as he was concerned, the race was over. He probably even thought he'd won. Carole didn't care what his motive was. She was just glad he'd stopped. Carole drew in Starlight's reins and rode over to Marie.

Marie didn't have the reins, and her feet were out of Patch's stirrups, but she was still in the saddle. She was leaning forward against Patch's neck, clutching it. Tears streaked her face. She gasped with the sobs that racked her body.

Carole dismounted. She took Patch's reins and Starlight's and walked the horses to a fence post nearby. She secured the reins around the pole.

"Come on," she said gently, helping Marie out of the saddle. "Let's get you down from there for a breather, okay?"

Without answering, Marie allowed Carole to help her down. Carole fished in the pocket of her breeches and found a rumpled handkerchief. She offered it to Marie. Marie wiped at her tears, but they kept coming. Carole led her to a small rock on the edge of the field, where they could sit and talk in peace. But first, Marie needed to cry.

Carole knew Marie wasn't just crying about the fright she'd had with Patch. Nor was she crying about Carole's deception. She was crying about everything awful that had happened to her in the last few months, but mostly about her father's death. Carole put her arm around her to comfort her.

"It's okay," Carole said. "I know. I really do. About the only thing I can tell you is that it will get better. That's not much comfort right now. Maybe that's one of the reasons I didn't tell you about my mother before. I knew it wouldn't help."

"How does it get better? It doesn't change," Marie said. "Nothing can change the fact that he's dead."

"I know," Carole said.

Marie's tears finally subsided. She blew her nose a final time. "Thank you," she said.

98

"For what?" Carole asked.

"For knowing how I feel. A lot of people kept telling me not to cry. You knew better. A lot of people told me that things would change. You knew better. A lot of people kept telling me how to feel. You didn't. You just let me feel what I felt. You knew you couldn't change that. You should have told me about your mother, but I guess I understand and, anyway, you didn't really lie."

"Sort of," Carole admitted.

"And mostly thank you for saving me when I let Patch run wild. That was scary!"

"You can say that again!"

Marie shivered with the memory and the girls laughed. It helped to release a lot of the fear they'd both had when Patch was on the run. They felt better when they were done laughing.

"Phew," Marie said. "Now what do we do?"

"Next, we get you back in the saddle and walk slowly and carefully back through the fields to Pine Hollow. And as we walk, I'll tell you more about how I felt when my mother died, if you want to hear it. I'll tell you how much I love horseback riding and what a comfort it was to me when I was saddest. It's still a comfort to me. Then I'll tell you I think you can get as much out of it as I do. And, finally, I'm going to try to talk you into joining our polocrosse team."

"Really? You think I'm good enough?"

Carole cocked her head as if she were thinking hard.

"Well," she began, "we lost our last game by about thirty points. I think that, with you on our team, we ought to be able to change the odds. This time, I hope we'll only lose by half that. Want to join up?"

"Sure," Marie said. "But it depends a bit on my mother."

"I've been meaning to speak to you about her," Carole began.

"LOOK AT THIS," Stevie announced in Pine Hollow's locker area eight days later. "My ankle is getting small enough now for me to put on my boots today!"

She displayed her new footwear for anybody who was interested.

"Is it still the awful orangey-purple color you tried to get us to look at last week?" Lisa asked.

"Nuh-uh," Stevie said. "I'm into green now. A nice sort of olive color, tinged with yellow."

"Gross!" Carole grimaced.

"Can I see it?" Adam Levine asked.

"It'll cost you a quarter," Stevie said. She'd found her natural-made color schemes were her main source of income these days, especially among her younger brother's friends. She was just trying it out on Adam.

"Forget it."

Stevie didn't mind. Unbandaging and rebandaging was a real nuisance. She'd want at least seventy-five cents for that.

"So, what techniques are we going to work on today, O master coach of polocrosse?" Carole asked, changing the subject. "After all, the rematch is tomorrow."

"Piece of cake," Stevie declared. She looked stern, but the fact was she was flattered that Carole had called her the master coach of polocrosse—even jokingly. They had had four practices since the last match and they were actually and truly getting better. Stevie was very proud of what they'd learned and accomplished.

She checked her list. "Today we're going to work on stealing the ball. And then, if we have time, dribbling, and then, we have to go over crossing fouls, and then we need to review goal shots."

"Ah, we're going to have a three-hour practice session!" Lisa said brightly.

Stevie tossed a bootjack at her. "No, you're safe there. Max showed me that the rules make it illegal for any horse to participate in more than fifty-four minutes of polocrosse a day. That should go for practices, too."

Marie finished tucking in her shirttails, took her boots out of her cubby, and sat down on the bench next to Stevie to put them on.

"Thanks," she said.

"For what?" Stevie asked.

"For letting me join up."

"I'm not sure we exactly *let* you join," Stevie said, musing about the situation. "I think the correct verb is shanghai."

Marie smiled. "Maybe," she said. "But I'm still glad you did it."

"Lisa and Carole and I are meeting after practice at TD's. Want to come along?"

"Great," Marie said. "I'll be there."

Stevie stood up then. "Practice begins in ten minutes. Get your horses ready, guys!" Then she picked up her crutches and headed for the playing field where they would practice. She wanted a few minutes to herself before they began.

Stevie had found that being a coach was very different from being a player. For one thing, she wasn't doing the exercises herself. She was telling the players what to do. She'd learned that if they found something hard to do, it was probably because it *was* hard, not because they weren't trying hard enough. She'd also learned a lesson in the first disastrous match against Cross County, and that was that yelling only made the team angry—at her. There had been lots of times in practices when she'd wanted to yell and scream, but the only time she had done it was when the riders were across the field and she didn't think they could hear her. For Stevie, that was a victory. She knew it and she was proud of it.

The other victory was that she had somehow convinced everybody that when it came to polocrosse, all she cared about was learning, having fun, and doing a better job than they had before. Still, in her own heart, her goal was to win, to beat Phil's team, to show him he wasn't the only hotshot polocrosse player in the state!

She could feel the excitement of the impending competition, but she wouldn't let it show. She couldn't even afford to think about it—or him. A few players approached the field, ready for practice. Stevie looked once again at her clipboard, concentrating on the practice in front of them, not the match tomorrow. "One day at a time," she told herself. "Just one."

AFTER PRACTICE, FOUR girls—The Saddle Club, plus Marie—walked over to TD's, chatting and giggling on the way.

"Look, Ma! No crutches! Not even a cane!" Marie said gleefully, showing her friends how well she could walk now. "My therapist says it's all because of the riding. It's made my legs a lot stronger."

"Riding has done some other things for you, too, I think," Lisa said.

"Sure has," Marie said. "It's given me a lot to think about, and it's been a lot of fun. I hadn't been letting myself have much fun."

"Not much that had been happening to you *was* much fun," Carole reminded her. "I mean, eight weeks flat on your back in a hospital isn't my idea of high comedy."

"Mine, either," Marie confirmed. "Anyway, I'm having fun now, and I'm glad to bequeath my crutches and my cane to Stevie!"

"Not me," Stevie said. "I'm almost ready to toss mine out, too. The doctor thinks I'll be rid of these things in another week. I think they're about ready to go now. Whenever it is, though, I'll be glad when that day comes."

"You won't either," Carole said. "When that happens, people will stop offering to help you—"

"Boys will stop offering to carry your books—"

"They never did that in the first place!" Stevie said. "They all just want to try my crutches!"

"Even Phil?" Lisa asked.

"Phil who?" Stevie said.

Carole and Lisa looked at each other, but they weren't sure they wanted to ask Stevie exactly what she meant. Still, friends were friends, and if it meant helping Stevie when she didn't think she needed help, well, then, that was what The Saddle Club was all about.

Carole found a booth for them at TD's and located a corner for Stevie's crutches. She sat down next to Marie, leaned forward with her elbows on the table, and looked straight at Stevie.

"Now," she began in her serious daughter-of-a-Marine-colonel voice. "Let's talk. Are you telling us that you've got some kind of problem with Phil Marston that we need to know about?"

Stevie couldn't hold it any longer. "The game is tomorrow. We're going to show him then. Really!"

"We thought you were over this," Carole said, surprised.

"And if you're not, you ought to have your head examined."

"Why? He's my boyfriend and if I want to have a fight with him, I will," Stevie said.

"Not that I'm so experienced, but it seems to me if you're going to have a fight with your boyfriend, it should be a fight that makes sense, don't you think so, Carole?" Lisa asked.

"I do. Besides, this isn't a fight. You're trying to prove something that doesn't need to be proven. You know what this reminds me of?" Carole asked Lisa. "It reminds me of the sort of unpredictable way my father gets worried about me. Your mother does the same thing. And so does Marie's mother. Only with Stevie, it's a sort of unpredictable competition with Phil."

"Stop talking about me as if I weren't here!" Stevie snapped at her friends.

What Carole wanted to tell Stevie was to start acting as if she were there. She was saved from saying something she would have been sorry for by the arrival of the waitress.

Lisa ordered chocolate yogurt with banana slices. Carole asked for hot fudge on vanilla ice cream. Marie ordered a dish of chocolate chip. The waitress then looked expectantly at Stevie, who was famous for her outrageous sundaes. She was not disappointed.

"I'll have chunky chewy chocolate, with walnuts, marshmallow, pineapple, and carob chips."

The waitress paled. She wrote the order quickly and disappeared.

"Oh, and a maraschino cherry on top!" Stevie called after her.

Carole, Lisa, and Marie all laughed. As long as Stevie could order such awful combinations, how could they stay angry with her?

12

THERE WAS A flurry of activity at Pine Hollow early the next morning. Since the return polocrosse match was to take place at Cross County's stable, all of the players' horses had to be loaded on vans for the ride over. Carole declared herself in charge of that.

"Horse's name?"

"Pepper," Lisa said, though she felt silly saying it, since Carole could look up and see which horse it was as easily as she could tell her.

"Saddle?"

"Check."

"Bridle?"

"Check."

"Grooming bucket?"

That was as much of that game as she wanted to play.

"Carole, I'm standing right here in front of you, holding a horse's lead rope, saddle, and bridle. How could I possibly have his grooming bucket, too?"

"Oh, yeah," Carole said, realizing how silly the question was. "Okay, so load him up and let me know when you've got his grooming bucket on board, okay?"

"Okay."

"Next!" Carole called out.

STEVIE WAS A mass of confused emotions. She was excited. She was nervous. She was even a little afraid. She wished she could play, but, in a way, she was relieved she couldn't. Her team would do fine. She knew that. But she didn't know if they would be able to win. One minute, she decided it didn't matter very much if they won. All they had to do was try their best. The next minute, she didn't feel that way at all. All she could think of then was how good it would feel to prove to Phil that her team was better than his. Or would it? She didn't know. And, with Carole and Max calling her at the same instant, she didn't have time to figure it out.

"Stevie, you've got to make sure we've got extra racquets and balls. If our equipment breaks, we could have to forfeit!"

"Stevie, did you call Cross County to find out where we should unload our horse vans?" Max asked.

"Extra racquets are in the storage bin in the first van," she told Carole. "Cross County says we have to unload behind their barn and we can use the paddock right there for our horses," she told Max. "Okay?"

"Okay," Carole said.

"Nice job," Max added.

And they were off.

WHEN THEY ARRIVED at Cross County, Stevie realized that she'd left her crutches at Pine Hollow. Although she had been putting weight on her foot, she wasn't sure how she'd do without anything to lean on.

Phil saw her sitting in the open door of the van, uncertainly contemplating the ground in front of her. "What's the problem?" he asked.

"I forgot my crutches," she told him.

"Here, I'll help you," he said.

He gave her a boost off of the van seat and helped her stand, allowing her to test putting some weight on the ankle.

"Okay?" he asked. She nodded. It hurt a little, but she thought she could walk. She reached forward with her sore ankle to step.

"Here, put your arm around my shoulder and lean on me," he suggested.

Stevie did that. She found, at first, that it seemed almost odd to walk without the crutches she'd gotten used to. But, with Phil's help, it was okay. He took her over to the edge of the playing field and found a seat for her where she could see everything that was going on.

"I've got to leave you now," he said. "But I'll see you later. And, good luck, okay?"

He leaned forward and kissed her softly on her cheek. Then he was gone.

What a nice guy, Stevie thought. *I'm really lucky to know somebody as nice as that.*

AS WITH THE last match, the players drew numbers and letters for their squads. Carole, Marie, and Lisa were Attack, Center, and Defense on the A squad. Adam, Betsy, and Polly were the B squad. Again, the match was to be four chukkas of six minutes each, with two minutes between the chukkas. The A squad would play the first and third chukkas. The B squad would play second and fourth.

Phil was on Cross County's B squad. Lisa was a little relieved that there would be no direct competition between The Saddle Club and Phil. When it came to competition with Phil, even indirect competition was as much as Stevie could stand!

Then Mr. Baker announced that play would begin in five minutes.

The teams rushed to finish tacking up their horses and checking their equipment. Lisa found the racquet she liked the best and located Carole's for her too. "Nervous?" she asked.

"A little," Carole said. "But not about the game. I'm nervous about Stevie!"

"Me, too," Lisa confessed. "Every time she gets this I'm-better-than-Phil bug, we seem to suffer. Remember how it was at riding camp?"

"Too well," Carole said. "So I guess we'd better get out there and win this one for the Gipper."

"The what?"

Watching old movies was one of Carole's favorite activities with her father. She sometimes forgot that not everybody had seen *The Knute Rockne Story*. "Some other time," she said. "Let's just say, for now, that we should do our best."

"It's a deal."

Carole helped Marie mount Comanche and they all did high fives. "High fifteen!" Carole announced. They were ready then.

The girls trotted onto the playing field and lined up next to the Cross County team. The Cross County A team looked curiously at Carole, Marie, and Lisa. Lisa had the funniest feeling they were licking their chops. There was no question that they'd enjoyed beating Horse Wise the last time. Lisa decided she'd do her best to see that they might not have as much fun this time!

"Begin play!" Mr. Baker announced, tossing the ball between the teams.

Lisa kept her eye on the ball as it came toward her. She reached out and up with her racquet, swiped at it, and was delighted to discover that she had actually caught the ball on the toss-in.

She heard Stevie cheer from the sidelines. Now, if only she could think what would be the right thing to do with the ball.

"Throw it here!" Marie called to her.

That made sense. Marie was down the field toward the goal they were shooting for. Lisa held her racquet firmly, took a swing, and the ball sailed out of her racquet—toward Marie, just like it was supposed to!

"Yeahhhhh!" Stevie yelled.

Marie reached out for the ball, but the toss was long and she couldn't get it. The Cross County Center picked it up. This called for some defense! Marie maneuvered Comanche over to face the Center's horse so she would pass him on his right side, where he carried his racquet. Marie felt like a jousting knight as she gave Comanche a signal to canter. She took aim when they neared the other rider, and she batted his racquet from below. The ball popped out. Marie caught it in midair.

"Raaaahhhhh!" Stevie yelled.

Marie spotted Carole nearby. She bounce-passed the ball over to her. Carole was near the penalty line. She couldn't carry the ball over it and Marie wasn't allowed to cross it. Marie rode Comanche right up to the line and waited. As Carole approached the line, she tossed the ball to Marie. Once she was over it, Marie tossed it back. Then, just as they had been practicing, Carole turned toward the goal, took aim, and tossed. The ball passed right between the goalposts.

"Score!" Mr. Baker called.

"Yippeeeeee!" yelled Stevie. So did all of the Horse Wise cheering section.

There wasn't time for congratulations, though, because play resumed right away. They lined up again. Cross County got the ball on the toss-in. Lisa went down to the goal area right away to protect against a scoring attempt. The Cross County team was good at passing the ball among themselves, but they couldn't move it down the field fast enough to escape the strong defense of Horse Wise. Carole and Marie worked together, and, when one pass went wild, Carole was the first to get to the loose ball. She scooped it up and headed back up the field toward the goal.

This time, Cross County stopped her in time. Their Attack hit her stick, and the ball bounced out-of-bounds. That meant another toss-in.

Nobody caught the ball. It bounced on the ground. There was a free-for-all as the players tried to pick it up. The result was that the ball got knocked out-of-bounds again. Once again, Mr. Baker tossed it in.

Carole caught it. She tilted her racquet, trying to trap the ball to defend against somebody hitting her racquet. She turned Starlight around and headed for the goal. She found herself being pursued by three players from Cross County—one of whom was their Defense player, who just wanted to beat Carole to the goal. The field was completely open ahead of her.

Carole saw the penalty line approaching and knew she couldn't carry the ball over herself. She looked around desperately, hoping to find Marie or Lisa there to help her out. The trouble was that Carole had gotten such a head start on everybody that not even her teammates were in the neighborhood. *Bounce it*, she told herself. It was the only way. She was going to have to bounce it on the ground and then pick it up on the other side of the line. It was sort of like dribbling in basketball, only on a moving horse, using a long-handled racquet, and it wasn't anywhere near as easy. Nevertheless, she didn't have a choice.

Carole adjusted the angle of her racquet, lifted the stick, turned it over, and tossed the ball out onto the ground as hard as she could. It smacked off the turf, sailed over the penalty line, and rose high into the air. Carole thought it was almost waiting for her as it floated. She flew over the penalty line after it, caught it in her racquet, and then immediately shot for the goal.

"Score!"

The only people more surprised than the Cross County Pony Clubbers were the Horse Wise Pony Clubbers.

"Yoweeeee!" cried Stevie.

The chukka was almost over by then, but there was enough time left for Cross County to score. Mr. Baker tossed in the ball. The Cross County Attack caught the ball on the fly and tossed it to their Center, who tossed it back to the Attack. The two of them played a game of keep-away as they rode down the field and, when the Attack crossed the penalty line, Lisa was waiting for them. She did everything she could to stop the ball from going in, but it wasn't enough.

"Score!"

Bzzzzzzp! The buzzer for the end of the chukka sounded.

Carole, Lisa, and Marie rode off the field triumphant. Their teammates greeted them and hugged them.

"Hey, guys, it's not over!" Carole reminded them. But as far as Lisa and Carole were concerned, the rest didn't matter. The fact was they were playing and they were giving Cross County a run for their money. That was what really mattered. The rest was just for fun.

Two minutes later, the second chukka started. Betsy and Polly were doing a fine job, but there was definitely something wrong with Adam. He was playing Center and he seemed to be almost out of it. He waved his racquet weakly at balls he ought to have caught, and once it seemed as if he was almost off-balance on his horse.

"What's the matter with him?" Carole asked.

"Look at him," Lisa said. "Unless my eyes deceive me, he's pale and sweaty and I don't think it's from playing polocrosse. Personally, I think he's sick."

"Sick?" Carole said, as if she'd never heard the word before. Then she looked for herself. Adam was definitely not feeling well. She nudged Stevie. "Look at Adam," she said. "He's sick."

"He will be when I'm through with him!" Stevie said through clenched teeth. "He just missed an easy pass and doesn't even seem to know which end of the field he's playing!"

"No, I mean, really. He's sick," Carole said. "Look at him. His color's all wrong and he's got this dizzy look—"

Bzzzzzzzp! The second chukka was over. The score was tied, 4–4.

"Time!" Max called. He, too, had seen that something was wrong with Adam. He ran over to the boy. "Adam," he called. "Are you okay?"

"I'll be fine," Adam protested, dismounting and landing on the turf with a thud. "I've just got to—"

He didn't finish his sentence. He just ran. His mother, who had come to watch the match, followed him as fast as she could. Mr. Baker pointed the way.

"Oh, poor Adam!" Lisa said.

"There's a bug that's been going around," Marie said. "He'll be okay in a couple of days."

"But he has to play again in just a few minutes!" Stevie said.

"Forget it!" Carole told her. "His mother will be taking him home in just a few minutes. He won't be back on a horse today."

An unhappy look crossed Stevie's face. "I'm going to

have to find a substitute for him—or we'll end up forfeiting."

"We don't have any substitutes," Lisa said. "All we have is us."

"Resume the game in one minute!" Mr. Baker announced.

"We've got to mount up!" Carole said. "Come on, team, let's do it!"

Stevie stood up from her chair and walked slowly toward the stable. She told Max she wanted to check on Adam. It wasn't quite the truth. She really wanted to do some thinking.

She saw Adam and Mrs. Levine climbing into her car. He still looked pale, but a little relieved.

"I'll see to his horse," Stevie assured the Levines.

"Thanks, and sorry," Adam said weakly.

Stevie shrugged. "You couldn't help it. You tried. Thanks for that."

The car doors slammed.

Adam's horse, Barq, was tied up to the fence by the stable entrance. She took his reins and patted his neck. She thought about what she was going to do.

She was going to take Adam's place. She had her boots on. If she could walk, she could ride. The trouble was she didn't know if she could play polocrosse. Her team was doing a wonderful job without her. What if she blew it for them?

Stevie sighed. Why did she always put herself into

these situations? Why was she always competing with Phil? What difference did it make? Was Phil competing with her? As she thought back on the things he'd done and said over the last few weeks, she couldn't honestly tell herself that Phil thought this was the same sort of contest between them that she'd been thinking it was.

At first, she'd wanted to beat him so badly, she'd hurt her friends' feelings and humiliated her teammates with an overwhelming defeat. Then, she'd been so determined to be the perfect polocrosse player that she'd hurt herself pretty badly. And then she'd tried another tack: She'd been the perfect coach. Well, actually, she'd been a pretty good coach. Her team was doing well. She was glad of that, but that wasn't quite the same thing as proving that she was better than Phil. If she got on the horse and took Adam's place, she'd be competing with Phil. And every second that she played, she might be wondering, *Which one of us is better?*

Who cared?

"Why so serious, Stevie?" It was Phil, as if on cue.

"I'm thinking," she said.

"About what?"

"About polocrosse," she told him. "I'm trying to decide if I should try to replace Adam in the next chukka. What do you think?"

"Can you ride?" he asked excitedly. "Is your ankle really healed enough?"

"I'm pretty sure I'd do okay on that score," Stevie said.

"I'm not sure my doctor would agree and I'm glad my parents aren't here to say no like they probably would. As far as I know, though, I could do it."

"So what's the problem, then? Do it."

It seemed so simple when he said it, but maybe he just didn't understand.

"It's not that. It's—well, how do you feel about it?"

"Me? I think it's great that you're feeling well enough to do it."

"How are you going to feel if we beat you?"

"Your team is much better than it was two weeks ago. I think there's a good chance you *will* beat us."

"Do you mind?"

"Losing isn't my favorite activity, but we're playing our best, so I can't complain."

"And what if I'm better than you are? Would you mind?"

He looked at her quizzically. "Is that what this is all about? Are you afraid I'm going to be better than you?"

"Partly," Stevie answered honestly.

"Or that you're better than I am and I'll be angry?"

"That, too," Stevie said. "I'm also afraid of how much I want to be better than you."

Phil smiled.

"You're a funny one, Stevie Lake," he said. "Maybe I am, too. We always want to be better than each other, don't we?" She nodded. "But when it comes right down to it, know what? As far as I'm concerned, deep down, where it's the most important, you always win with me."

"I do?"

"Yes, you do," he said. Then, as if to prove that he meant it, he kissed her. And she kissed him back.

"Will you kiss me again if you lose?" she asked.

"Of course I will. And if you lose, you're going to have to kiss me. Okay?"

"It's a deal," Stevie said, her mind now made up.

She unhitched Adam's horse's reins and walked with Phil back to the playing field.

13

"PLEASE, MAX, PLEASE!" Stevie said. "It's only six minutes. How bad can it be? Look, I feel fine; I got into the saddle without any trouble. Barq and I are getting along fine, no trouble—isn't that right, boy?" Barq, an Arabian horse with a sweet disposition, remained quiet.

"I don't know, Stevie," Max said.

"Just six minutes, Max—"

"Oh, all right."

Max arranged for the substitution with Mr. Baker. The Cross County team had no objection, so Stevie was approved as the B team's Center.

This was the final chukka of the match. Stevie had completely missed the third chukka, when the A teams were playing. She'd been with Phil. She had no idea what the score was and the field had no scoreboard. She was too embarrassed to ask anybody. Besides, she reminded herself, the score didn't matter. What mattered was playing as well as she could, and having a good time.

"Begin play!" Mr. Baker announced. He threw the ball to the players.

Stevie reached up for it. She didn't even come close. From behind her, she heard a racquet whiz through the air and a triumphant, "I've got it!" The voice was Phil's.

As soon as she knew Cross County had possession, that meant she had two jobs. The first was to do everything she could to keep them from moving the ball down the field toward the goal. The second was to try to get it away from them.

Stevie now knew an awful lot about polocrosse. She had had to learn everything she could in order to teach her teammates. But learning was very different from doing. Just as the racquet had felt unfamiliar and cumbersome in her hand, the task ahead of her seemed strange as well.

"Let's go!" Polly called. It was just what Stevie needed.

Stevie spun Barq around to pursue Phil. He had slowed down, looking for a teammate to pass the ball to so he could cross the penalty line. His teammates were both out of position. Stevie, on the other hand, was nearby.

She rode up behind him, swung her stick over to her left side—his right—and swiped upward, jostling the ball out of his racquet.

"Hey!" he yelled, but the ball had landed right by Stevie's horse. She leaned over, scooped it up, and headed down the field.

Soon, she was the one being pursuéd. There, in front of her, was Polly, their Attack. Polly crossed the penalty line. Stevie passed the ball to her. Polly didn't catch it, but she picked it up before the Cross County Defense could get to it. Then, with a big grin on her face, Polly threw the ball between the goalposts.

"Score!" Mr. Baker called out.

Stevie knew that, as a player, she wasn't supposed to yell and scream with joy when her team scored, but inside she was cheering like mad. She was happy about the point, that was for sure, but it wasn't the point that was making her the happiest. It was the teamwork. She and her teammates were working together. They were using the skills they had worked on so hard, and they were applying them to the strategies they'd been practicing. Each player had a different job and was doing it right.

"Go team!" Stevie whispered to herself.

Mr. Baker tossed the ball in for the next round of play. This time, things didn't go so easily for either side. They fought hard over the ball, tossing it, passing it, bouncing it, and stealing it. It changed possession three times before getting *near* one of the penalty lines and then flew out-of-bounds when Phil hit Stevie's racquet.

"Touché!" he said, grinning at her.

She had the funniest feeling he was thinking about collecting on their bet. So was she.

Mr. Baker announced that there were only forty-five seconds left in the chukka. Then he tossed the ball in a final time.

Forty-five seconds? Where had the time gone, Stevie wondered. The six minutes were absolutely flying by. Betsy picked up the ball this time and passed it to her. Stevie took it and began riding down the field toward their goal. There were hoofbeats coming up behind her. She looked for somebody to pass the ball to because she knew she'd be attacked in just a second. Neither Polly nor Betsy was anywhere in sight. Stevie had to do something. As long as she was carrying the ball like that, she was too vulnerable to having her stick hit.

Stevie decided to pass to herself. She bounced the ball on the ground ahead of her and then had Barq dash to catch up with it. It worked. She tried again. Once again, it worked. Then, out of nowhere, Phil appeared. He came right up next to her and tried to scoop the ball when she bounced it.

He missed it, but then so did she. They both scrambled to pick up the loose ball.

Bzzzzzzzp!

The game was over.

From both sides of the field, the Pony Clubbers, parents, and parent volunteers cheered loudly. Both teams had done a wonderful job and the match had been exciting from the first toss-in.

Stevie felt in a daze. She walked Barq over to the edge of the playing field and let Max help her down out of the saddle.

"You did a terrific job," he told her. "I'm really proud of what you did, both as a coach and a substitute player. Stevie, one thing I know about you—when you put your mind to getting something done, you really do it. Of course, I don't always approve of your methods, but then, I'm not complaining about results, am I?"

Max wasn't one to throw compliments around. Stevie knew he meant it and she was glad to hear his words.

"You're wonderful!" Carole shrieked, hugging her next. Stevie hugged back and hugged Lisa and Marie, as well as Polly and Besty when they all joined in.

"We're all wonderful!" Stevie said. "Aren't we?"

Everyone could agree on that.

"Uh, Stevie, could I talk to you for a moment, in private?" Phil asked. "It's about our bet. Remember?" he whispered in her ear.

"Oh, yes. Excuse me, guys. I'll be back in a few minutes."

She secured Barq to the fence and followed Phil to the far side of the stable building. She even let him help support her as she walked.

When they were sure they were out of sight of the excited crowds, Stevie turned to face Phil. She put her arms up around his neck and stood on her tiptoes as high as her sore ankle would allow. He encircled her with his arms, and leaned down. Then, to alleviate further strain on her ankle, he picked her up. Their lips met.

Kissing Phil was just plain wonderful as far as Stevie was concerned and this time was no exception. He held her tightly and warmly for a few more seconds. Then they kissed again and he put her back down on the ground.

"Hey, that was a great bet," Stevie said. "We'll have to do that again more often!"

Phil grinned. His green eyes sparkled. She loved it when he looked at her that way.

"Just one thing, though," Stevie said.

"What's that?"

"Who won?"

Phil began laughing.

"What's so funny?" she asked.

"I was just about to ask you the same thing!"

14

"YOU WERE GREAT!" Carole told Stevie. Lisa nodded agreement.

"So were you two," Stevie said. "And I realized the whole thing was about teamwork, right guys?"

The three of them were sitting at their favorite table at TD's, talking about The Game. They still all felt the thrill of their success.

"I can't believe how good it was to be playing together."

"It's what you taught us," Lisa said. "You were a really good coach."

The waitress arrived then. "The usual?" she asked. She disappeared before they could even answer.

"What do you suppose that means?" Lisa asked.

Carole and Stevie shrugged. "I guess we'll see soon enough," Stevie said.

"What were you and Max talking about on the way home in the van? You were yakking away in the front seat about something, but I just couldn't hear what it was," Lisa said.

"Oh, we were discussing our future tournament schedule. See, there are a couple of other Pony Clubs in the area, and some 4-H's, too, that might have polocrosse teams. I wanted to know what he thought about having a full-blown invitational tournament."

"And what did he say?" Carole asked.

"He said we ought to have more players on our team before we do that so that if somebody gets sick, we won't have to find some poor girl, still on crutches, to fill in for that person."

"Makes sense to me," Carole said.

"Don't worry," Lisa said. "Polocrosse is a lot of fun and pretty soon a lot of people are going to know about it and will be dying to play. We won't have any trouble expanding our team. You'll see."

The waitress approached the table, balancing a tray above her shoulder.

"Now, first, I thought you might want to try the banana frozen yogurt with honey." She placed the dish in front of Lisa.

"Looks good," Lisa said.

"And, I decided that caramel topping on chocolate ice cream was for you." That was for Carole.

"Interesting," Carole said.

"For you, we have something extremely exotic: a dish of vanilla."

She lowered the plate in front of Stevie, who couldn't hide her disappointment, until the waitress finished her description: "And strawberry, and bubble gum royale, with a Turkish-taffy topping, and peanut-crunch bits."

"Oh, wow!" Stevie said, obviously delighted at the waitress's idea of "the usual."

"Enjoy," the woman said. She left.

Carole leaned forward on the table and spoke conspiratorially to her friends. "I think she's hiding behind the pillar there," she said.

"Whatever for?" Stevie asked.

"To see if you will actually eat it."

"I will," Stevie promised. "Every last bite of it. Unless you guys want a taste. You're welcome, you know." She offered them the dish.

"No thanks," they said at once. All of them picked up their spoons then and began eating "the usual."

"Speaking of thanks, wasn't Marie just great today?" Lisa asked.

"Yes, she was," Carole said. "See how much riding has done for her? I just knew it would."

"And how is our little distraction plot coming along?" Stevie asked.

"Well, my father and her mother had a real date one night this week. I got the impression that Dad thinks Mrs. Dana is pretty cool."

"Do you suppose that's why he tried to put two halters on one horse today?" Lisa asked. "Now *that's* what I call distracted!"

"And speaking of distracted," Carole said, changing the subject, "what was all that stuff Phil was whispering to you today after the game?"

Stevie realized she hadn't told her friends about what had been going on between her and Phil. She left out a few personal details, but she brought them up-to-date on the things they needed to know.

"Boy, The Saddle Club is really something," Lisa said.

"How's that?"

"Well, in a few short weeks, we help rehabilitate a girl who's been in a car accident, we dabble in matchmaking, we learn a whole new sport, and we patch up a quarrel between Stevie and Phil. We sure did a lot, didn't we?"

"We sure did," Stevie agreed. "Now, I'm going to ask you guys to tell me something, honestly."

"What's that?" Carole asked.

Stevie looked at each of her friends. She was obviously uncomfortable with the question.

"Go ahead. Ask. What is it?" Lisa encouraged her.

"Tell me who won the game today?"

"You really don't know?"

Stevie shook her head.

Lisa and Carole looked at each other and broke into laughter. "She's recovering," Lisa said. "Definitely improved!"

"So?" Stevie persisted.

"It was a tie. Six to six."

Stevie grinned. "Here's to everybody, then," she said, raising her water glass in a toast.

"But mostly, here's to us," Carole added. Their glasses clinked. Some water even spilled on Stevie's sundae, but Stevie assured them she wouldn't notice the additional flavor.

ABOUT THE AUTHOR

BONNIE BRYANT is the author of more than forty books for young readers, including novelizations of movie hits such as *Teenage Mutant Ninja Turtles* and *Honey, I Shrunk the Kids*, written under her married name, B. B. Hiller.

Ms. Bryant began writing The Saddle Club in 1986. Although she had done some riding before that, she intensified her studies then and found herself learning right along with her characters Stevie, Carole, and Lisa. She claims that they are all much better riders than she is.

Ms. Bryant was born and raised in New York City. Her husband and sometime coauthor, Neil Hiller, died in 1989. She lives in Greenwich Village with her two sons.

YOUR PONY

A Young Person's Guide to Buying, Keeping and Riding Ponies

by Michael and Marilyn Clayton

Do you know how to look after a pony properly? Where to keep it, and how to feed it? How to jump a combination fence — or how to ride safely on the roads?

All the answers to all your questions about owning and riding a pony can be found in this invaluable guide that's full of sound advice and practical information on how to get the very best out of owning a pony — from choosing your first ever pony, to learning how to canter, gallop and jump, and all the fun you and your pony can have taking part in competitions.

Fully illustrated with photographs and line drawings.

SBN 185225 1263
£12.99 hardback

PARTRIDGE PRESS

We hope you enjoyed reading this book. If you would like to receive further information about available titles in the Bantam series, just write to the address below, with your name and address: Kim Prior, Bantam Books, 61-63 Uxbridge Road, Ealing, London W5 5SA.

If you live in Australia or New Zealand and would like more information about the series, please write to:

Sally Porter
Transworld Publishers
(Australia) Pty Ltd
15-23 Helles Avenue
Moorebank
N.S.W. 2170
AUSTRALIA

Kiri Martin
Transworld Publishers (NZ) Ltd.
Cnr. Moselle and Waipareira Avenues
Henderson
Auckland
NEW ZEALAND

All Bantam and Young Adult books are available at your bookshop or newsagent, or can be ordered at the following address: Corgi/Bantam Books, Cash Sales Department, PO Box 11, Falmouth, Cornwall TR10 9EN.

Please list the title(s) you would like, and send together with a cheque or postal order. You should allow for the cost of the book(s) plus postage and packing charges as follows:
80p for one book
£1.00 for two books
£1.20 for three books
£1.40 for four books
Five or more books free.

Please note that payment must be made in pounds sterling; other currencies are unacceptable.

(The above applies to readers in the UK and Republic of Ireland only)

BFPO customers, please allow for the cost of the book(s) plus the following for postage and packing: 80p for the first book, and 20p for each additional copy.

Overseas customers, please allow £1.50 for postage and packing for the first book, £1.00 for the second book, and 30p for each subsequent title ordered.

THE SADDLE CLUB

Bonnie Bryant

Share the thrills and spills of three girls drawn together by their special love of horses in this adventurous series.

PEN PALS

by Sharon Dennis Wyeth

How do four boy-crazy girls meet four girl-crazy boys? They place an ad for PEN PALS, of course! Well, that's what Lisa, Shanon, Amy and Palmer (otherwise know as the Foxes) do — and it's not long before they get a reply!

It all started with
the

SWEET VALLEY TWINS

Follow the adventures of Jessica, Elizabeth and all their friends at Sweet Valley as twelve-year-olds. A super series with one new title every month!